SURPRISE BATTLE

A Different Outcome

Second Edition

Thomas Trimble

(2-3)

Surprise Battle Copyright © 2020 Thomas Trimble

Cover designed by:

Diana TC

Book Cover Designer

Triumph Book Covers

www.triumphbookcovers.com

This book is a work of historic, sci-fi, fiction. Names, characters, places, and incidents either are products of the author's imagination or are used fictitiously. Any resemblance to actual persons, living or dead, events, or locales is entirely coincidental.

PREFACE

This book is an Alternate History of Naval War, Sci-Fi. It is a historical World War II fiction loosely based on events that took place in the Pacific, before and during the landings at Guadalcanal. To keep a logical flow, it uses real references to events and ships but has taken them into this fictional world I created. Many conditions are different from real technical Navy operations and the structure of the boat, veterans please just accept that as part of the science fiction.

As I wrote this book, my thoughts were focused on my deep appreciation for the brave men and women of our armed services at any time and generation.

The fictional military actions in this book created situations where many people who perished in that military struggle would have survived. I wish it were true and they could help with this book. My sincere thanks to them all for giving us our freedom.

I want to offer my thanks to my group of editors and Beta readers who have helped to polish this story to help it flow and at least be believable in the fictional world. I also want to thank Diana from Triumph Book Covers for designing the great cover.

Enjoy **SURPRISE BATTLE: A Different Outcome**.

NEW SUBMARINE

August 1, 2025, Time 08:10, 100 miles

East of Taiwan

The bright sun shines down on the vast Pacific Ocean as a silent behemoth lurks below the surface. This giant is the SSN-809 the USS Joseph Kane. A new and highly technically advanced Virginia Class Nuclear Attack Submarine. The almost four-hundred-foot-long submarine was named after Alfred Joseph Kane, a Fleet Admiral in the Pacific during WWII. This is actually the second ship named to honor this famous sailor. The first was a Farragut Class Guided Missile Destroyer simply named USS Kane. The USS Kane was scrapped in 1994.

The USS Joseph Kane is the latest Virginia Class variant out of the shipyard in 2025. It is equipped with several new and unique features. One is a section of the boat called the Virginia Payload Module or VPM. This module allows the ship to launch various weapons vertically, the biggest of them the

Tomahawk land-attack cruise missile. The other new feature is a module that gives them a rear torpedo room and a raised area on the hull where the torpedoes can be launched on either side of the tail. This returns to the design of submarines in the early 20th century where all boats had rear tubes. It was decided that this gives them an extra advantage in addition to the four tubes in the bow. This is only possible since there is no propeller because of a silent Propulsor drive.

This new war machine is under the command of Captain Walter Richey. He is standing his watch at the electronic command center. This tall trim man with graying brown hair is illuminated in the light from the huge array of LCD displays used for a multitude of functions in the Control Room. From his command position, he directs the crew of 136 and looks at the young fresh-faced sailors and officers who are running his boat. It makes him remember his early naval days, some 18 years ago just after graduating from the Naval Academy. It makes him think how wonderful it is to have this prestigious command. About 8 years later he married his wife Jean they don't have any children. Not because they don't want any but more because of his constant deployments.

After 3 years of intense training at sea, he became a submarine captain. His first command, if you can call it that, was a left-over Los Angles Class Boat (688 type) with a minimum crew which was quickly retired of old age, but retains a place in his heart as his first command. Then there was his deployment on the USS Minnow which in 2015 almost sank off the coast of San Diego. Massive flooding caused a major electrical short and fires. The crew had to abandon the boat as it began to list and started to sink. Thanks to the work of the crew and other nearby Navy vessels he was able to escape the ship relatively unharmed physically but the scars of that day will always be ingrained in the back of his mind. From that day forth Captain Richey has learned the importance of paying close attention to everything going on in his boat. Watch the details.

Kane's current deployment is an active patrol of the Asia Pacific area, near the East China Sea. Tensions have been escalating between North Korea and China. Sometimes it seems like the U.S. Government is poking them both with sticks to see who will flinch first. They are currently patrolling an area south of the East China Sea, approximately 100 miles east of Taiwan, providing overwatch in the area to be sure they are close if problems erupt.

The Communications Officer is Lieutenant Martin Williams, they call him Denzel because of his rugged good looks. Of course, he would say he isn't just a pretty face but he has a great mind too, and his Master's degree in System Engineering from Johns Hopkins and a BS in Electronics from the Naval Academy seem to prove that. But the thing that makes him most proud is the fact that he was the first person in his family to go to college, let alone Annapolis. His family were poor farmers in Virginia, working the same lands that his once slave ancestors had worked before the Civil War.

The Lieutenant was handed an urgent message from the radioman and immediately called the Conn.

"Conn, Communications Officer. Sir, we have received an urgent message on the extremely low-frequency system from COMSUBPAC."

"Captain, Aye. Bring the message to the Conn."

"Radio. Aye."

A young sailor, Ensign Able ran into the Conn. He was holding the bright yellow paper with the urgent message and handed it to the Captain, quickly turned and left. The message was:

"08/1/2025 08:10

To: Captain Richey, CO KANE,

Captain, a submarine with a previously unlisted sonar signature has been tracked leaving the underground submarine base, Sanya Naval Base, located on the south-east coast of the Hainan Island. Intelligence reports this submarine is a new experimental variant of the Chinese Type 039A a Yuan-class Nuclear Missile Submarine capable of launching intercontinental ballistic missiles. Your orders are to acquire their position as they leave Hainan Island and trail this Chinese submarine and observe its operation. Do not track further east than Bikini Atoll. If they proceed beyond that point, break trail and notify COMSUBPAC of their last know position. Pearl will take over the tracking. Proceed with caution, avoid any incidents, and do not engage unless fired upon. A special security update has been sent via satellite.

Admiral John Rankin, COMSUBPAC, Pearl Harbor, HI"

All the Captain could think was, "Great we are going to play chase the mouse across the Pacific."

Grabbing the PA mike, he said, "XO to the Conn!"

In a flash, Lieutenant Commander Michael Mascoll appeared in the Conn. He is a ten-year navy man. He moved quickly through the officer's training and qualifications for the various positions on a Nuclear submarine, to now be the XO.

"XO reporting as ordered, Sir."

"XO, we have just received new orders from COMSUBPAC, what do you think of this?", as he handed the XO the printout.

"Sir looks like we have a new Chinese Boomer coming out of their barn to play in the Pacific."

"XO, get the download and take us to find this boat. You have the Conn."

"Aye, XO has the Conn."

The XO is short in stature, but a very muscular and commanding presence. He is also a respected officer and an excellent interface to the entire crew. He has been a friend and trusted officer to the Captain for 5 years.

The XO grabbed the PA mike to say,

"Comm Officer, XO."

"Williams, Aye."

"Mr. Williams access the COMSUBPAC database and download the file on this latest Yuan class submarine and transfer it up to the Conn."

"Have it to you in two minutes, XO."

"Navigator, Conn."

"Navigator, Aye."

"Plot us a course to where the Yuan would be leaving Hainan Island out into the Pacific."

"Conn, Navigator. Recommend course 1-8-5. We are 176 miles from the new operating area. They are 1088 miles from there and should arrive in approximately 39 hours."

"Conn, Aye."

The Chief of the Boat is Master Chief Jimmy Mack. He is 38 years old, a twenty-year Navy man and has served on almost every type of ship. He says he loves the Nuclear Submarines the most. The COB is the direct interface between the officers and the enlisted men who are controlling the boat. The COB would be the Diving Officer in charge of the pilots.

The XO orders, "OOD, steer course 1-8-5, make your speed 28 knots, depth 400 feet.".

Meanwhile, the Captain walked over to the Sonar station and said, "Seaman Billings"

"Aye Captain"

"We are about to start following a brand-new Yuan Class submarine that is headed due east out of Hainan Island. We are heading south about 176 miles to meet them as they come out into the Pacific. As soon as we are close enough, I need you to find that boat so we can get a trail."

Seaman Billings is a good old southern boy about 21 years old. He responded with the drawl in his voice, "No problem sir. I'll find them and they won't even know where we all are. Just like hunting possum. The ocean is my woods and I can always hear the animals moving."

"How many Yuans do we have in the computer right now?"

"Currently 7 in the computer, Sir."

"Designate this knew one 'Yuan 8' and get me a track as soon as you find her."

"I won't let you down, Sir."

"Seaman Billings, I am counting on that. Thanks."

"Aye, Captain."

KANE glided away toward the south to a position where it could hunt for Yuan 8. The Captain went back to the Conn to discuss the data file they received.

The control room in KANE is like a modern computer room far more advanced than older boats like a Los Angeles Class submarine. Over 40 LCD monitors line the walls and work stations. The command station is a new all-electronic command center. Able to access many of the onboard systems including the Photonics array. One side of the room has a large navigation plot display table. The whole room looks like a swarm of lightning bugs on a hot summer night, with all the LEDs flashing on equipment. Eight crewmen of various ranks and with different functions man all of this equipment.

"Captain has the Conn."

"XO what was the data we received on this girl?"

"Captain, this is kind of second-hand information from Navy Intelligence."

The Captain chuckled, "Sometimes, Navy Intelligence is a conflict in terms."

"Sir, the summary of the information is that this new experimental variant of the Chinese Type 039A Yuan-class Nuclear Missile Submarine is suspected of being capable of launching intercontinental ballistic missiles. However, the intelligence information says that the Chinese missile program has not kept up with the submarine program so they don't have a missile that could reach the US from their home waters. This Yuan is said to be about the same size and speed as our boat. They believe it is equally as stealthy and technically advanced. We are to verify and record its capability."

The Captain said quietly to the XO, "First we play the submariner's waiting game. Take us to the operating area recommended by the Navigator. Submerge to 165 feet and do a slow patrol. Sonar will be watching for them. I will relieve you later."

"Aye, Sir. XO has the Conn."

FOLLOW THAT SUBMARINE

August 2, 2025, Time 17:57, 8 Miles North of the

line due east of Hainan Island

After the XO and Captain have rotated some downtime, they are both in the Conn with the OOD, for the task of finding their new prey. They have been on station in the new operating area for about 3 hours after a trip south. Sitting very quietly at 165 feet.

"Captain has the Conn."

The Officer of the Deck is Lieutenant Sam Martin. He is 30 years old, a ten-year Navy man, and has served on almost every type of ship as he quickly works his way up. He is heading quickly for XO and then Captain, fast tracking all the necessary qualifications.

"Conn, Sonar."

"Conn, Aye. What do you have?"

"Captain, I have a sub bearing 2-2-5, range about 7 miles."

"Sonar, any indication they hear us?"

"Sir, they are moving at 24 knots and at that speed, they have a low probability of detecting us."

"Sonar let us know when they have crossed in front of us."

"Sonar, Aye."

"OOD rig the ship for Ultra Quiet."

In about 30 minutes, "Conn, Sonar."

"Conn, Aye. What do you have?"

"Sir, they are now bearing 1-7-5, range about 8 miles and widening, they are still on course 0-9-0 at a depth of 350 feet. I have recorded a sonar signature for Yuan 8 as they passed. Now the computer can track them.".

"Conn, Aye."

The Captain announced, "OOD, rig the ship for Patrol Quiet."

The Captain says, "OOD, steer course 0-9-2, make your speed 25 knots, depth 450 feet. We are going to stay under them and slightly behind to gather data."

In a few minutes, sonar gave this update, "Conn, Sonar."

"Conn, Aye. What do we have?"

"Sir, it appears they are running some speed tests, they have accelerated quickly to 29 knots."

"Officer of the Deck, continue to match speed with them and assume a parallel course about 5 miles away and 100 feet deeper. Be sure we are recording everything they are doing."

"OOD, Aye."

♦ ♦ ♦

August 3, 2025, Time 02:57, 19 miles West of the Bikini Atoll

After 58 hours of shadowing the Chinese boat, they have learned a lot about it. First, it is nowhere near as stealthy as KANE because sonar can keep a constant track on it. Once they got the sonar signature for 'Yuan 8' the computer has been able to plot a track on it the entire time. It appears that at the same distance they can't hear KANE. It is also not as fast because their speed runs were maxed at about 29 knots and KANE was keeping up easily. It does seem to have similar basic capabilities to the Virginia Class boats.

This has been a long and somewhat boring trip in the Pacific, but orders are orders. Sonar has monitored the Chinese boat running those speed and diving drills and even an Emergency Blow where they breached the surface and shot the bow up what sonar estimated as 40 feet, splashing back down hard onto the surface. A really boring time playing chase the mouse, until right now.

The XO on the PA said urgently, "Captain to the Conn!"

Captain Richey hurried from his cabin to the Control Room. The OOD said, "Captain has the Conn."

Then the Captain asked, "XO what is the problem?"

"Sir, sonar reads the Chinese boat at a depth of 100 feet and he believes it has opened a couple of its missile doors."

"XO, thanks. I don't think there is anything for us to do until we know what they're doing."

"Conn, Sonar."

"Sonar, Aye."

"Captain, they have launched a missile!"

"Sonar what is our distance to them?"

"Sir, right before the launch they turned away from us, about 9.4 miles right now."

The Captain looked over to the XO and said quietly, "You think they would see the masts?"

The XO responded, "I don't think so, but we have to track that missile.".

"I agree, Commander."

The Captain ordered, "Officer of the Deck, Man battle stations, hold current course and speed, make your depth 90 feet and raise the masts."

"Aye, Captain."

A very loud claxon rang throughout the Boat and the OOD announced, "All hands man your Battle Stations! This is not a drill, repeat this is not a drill.".

The crew scrambled to their assigned positions, they have practiced these hundreds of times and do it without really thinking about it.

The Virginia Class submarines utilize two Photonics Masts replacing the traditional periscope. The masts contain high-resolution cameras, light intensification, and infrared sensors and an infrared laser range finder along with all the high-tech radio and radar antennas. All that input is displayed on LCD screens in the control room command center and a photonics station. As the boat nears the surface, the masts pop through to expose all the technical tracking equipment.

"Conn, Radar. Can you get a location and direction for that missile?"

"Aye Captain, it is heading due north, about 17 miles out from us, does not appear to be aimed at any strategic target."

"Captain, Aye."

The Captain asked, "XO, your opinion do you think we need to take any action?".

"No Sir other than just stay with them. That shot was not at anyone. We recorded a bit of information about it, got some video, that's all we can do."

"I agree."

There was a swell of tension in the control room as all the sailors realized that they are a few miles from a Chinese submarine that may have just launched a ballistic missile. No one knows where the next one might be aimed.

"Conn, Radar."

"Radar, Aye."

"Sir, the missile appears to have self-destructed. It started to lose altitude and then just disappeared."

"Conn, Sonar."

"Sonar, Aye."

"Captain, they have closed the missile doors and submerged to 375 feet. They have turned northward on a course to return to their base."

"Conn, Aye."

"Navigator, Conn."

"Navigator, Aye."

"Navigator, where the heck are we, after all this chasing around?"

"Sir, we are approaching south-west of Bikini Atoll."

The boat is currently at the easternmost point of the area they were instructed to track that Chinese submarine marked by the Bikini Atoll. Luckily, the Chinese boat has turned back.

♦ ♦ ♦

Bikini Atoll is actually, a coral reef in the Marshall Islands consisting of 23 islands in a circle surrounding a 229.4-square-mile lagoon. A onetime rich farming community on a Pacific paradise; now turned deadly by the abuse of humans, American humans. Now infamous for its history in US Nuclear Bomb testing starting during WWII. Bikini Atoll was selected for Nuclear Weapons testing during 1946, 1954, 1956, and 1958. The residents of the area were told to evacuate and the Navy helped them do that, but some stayed behind. Those tests consisted of air burst, land burst, and underwater tests. More than 170 Megatons of explosive power were detonated, releasing all forms of radiation contamination. Compare that to the 15 Kilotons used to eliminate Hiroshima.

♦ ♦ ♦

"Navigator, Conn."

"Navigator, Aye."

"Plot a course back to our original operating area near the East China Sea."

"Captain, recommend course 2-7-1."

"OOD, take a wide turn north-west to be sure we are far enough behind that Chinese sub and steer course 2-7-1, make your speed 25 knots, depth 400 feet.

"OOD, Aye."

"Radio, Conn."

"Radio, Aye."

"Send this message on a coded channel to Pacific Sub Command and include our recorded data in an encrypted file:

To: COMSUBPAC, Pearl Harbor 8/4/2025 20:03

KANE has shadowed the prototype Chinese submarine as far as the area near Bikini Atoll. The submarine ran a number of tests including the launch of a Ballistic Missile. The missile was destructed after about 10 miles. The boat has turned to return home. Following at a distance. Encrypted data from the investigation is being forwarded.

> *Captain Walter Richey, Commanding KANE."*

"Radio, Aye."

The control room is normally a calm place, kind of low-light with just the glow of all the computer screens. All of the sailors doing their assigned job with the Officer of the Deck or OOD directing the activity and executing the operational orders.

That noted calm of control was just about to be disturbed in a big way!

THE EVENT

August 5, 2025, Time 05:55, Near the Bikini Atoll

in the Pacific

In the Pacific Ocean on another hot August day. The sun has only been up an hour and the outside temperature reads 90 degrees with humidity to match. The USS Joseph Kane has just completed a mission to trail and gather information on a Chinese prototype submarine.

They are currently near Bikini Atoll. They are going to head back to their original operating area still tracking the Chinese submarine.

"Conn, Sonar!"

"Sonar, what do you have?".

The voice on the PA had a great urgency to it, "Captain, we are picking up a loud hum with a static crackle to it. It is overpowering everything else I was hearing.".

"Sonar, what does the computer say about it?"

"Just that Sir, high energy field, dead ahead, 3000 yards and closing fast."

"Officer of the Deck, make your depth 90 feet and raise the masts.

"Aye, Captain."

The OOD reported, "Captain, masts raised."

"Aye."

"Photonics, what is making that awful noise?"

"Captain, we see a bright blue wall of light with what looks like lightning in it. Our measurement says it's a quarter-mile across, twenty feet high and it looks like it extends below the surface. It appears to be moving right to left as if what we are seeing is just the front of a clockwise circulation. The leading edge is now, 1000 yards away and closing."

The Captain yelled, "Pilot steer course 2-2-0."

"Aye Sir. New course 2-2-0."

In another very shaky voice, "Conn, Pilot!"

"Pilot, what's wrong?".

"Sir, we can't change course. We have also increased to 20 knots without changing anything."

"OOD, All Stop immediately!"

The COB said, "Maneuvering is answering All Stop but we are still going 20 knots and increasing slowly.".

"Conn, Sonar."

"Go ahead Sonar."

"Sir we are now 500 yards from the energy field and closing."

Privately the Captain said, "OOD should we try back emergency?".

"No Sir, I don't think we could fight it and it would be a huge strain on the boat."

The Captain said, "OOD retract the masts."

It was a matter of a minute until all power in the boat flashed off. The normally bright control areas are no longer illuminate by the terminals. Every control station is black, even emergency lighting is only partially working, just the battle lanterns. Like the inside of a very big, dark closet with one little light bulb working.

Suddenly, a bright wall of transparent blue light. Like a knife blade with lightning type sparks in it, making a loud crackling hum came from the bow area. It entered the control room and slowly moved toward the stern. It looked like the boat was in a giant scanner as the beam moved across. As the crewman were covered by the blue wave they would yell and then vanish.

After the Captain was covered by the wave, he felt a kind of burning tingle, he seemed to be pulled in and in a second, he was standing right in the same spot. The crewmen hit before him were back in their places and the people more to the stern were gone. In a couple of minutes, the boat had cleared the field, all the people were back in their position, the lights and equipment came back on and everything rebooted.

The Captain looked around control, and out loud ask, "Is everyone alright?"

The crew members were kind of shaken but everyone said they were fine.

Down in the Engineering area, the Engineering Officer Lieutenant Commander Scotty Brown is just trying to clear his head and get his men to give him a status of all the systems. He is a 10-year submarine engineer. Trained and experienced in all the technology of nuclear reactors, submarine power systems, and general operation. He had never seen this one before.

The lights and the whole system flashed back on. The Captain hit the PA button so everyone could hear and said, "Engineering, what happened?"

Commander Brown said, "Sir we have no idea. The reactor is operating normally, the turbine generators is in operation but the load on it went through the roof. We have no idea where the power went, but we were all scanned by a blue energy wave. Several main breakers have tripped, we are closing them in now. We are continuing to investigate, that is all we have, Sir."

As soon as everything rebooted the Captain said, "OOD, raise the Photonics Masts.".

The CO looked at the Photonic Masts displays on his command center and saw nothing but the wall of that field of bright blue and sparks. Just like what had scanned through control. Nothing else was visible, off the stern. Infrared looked like just lightning on a black background. The bow was now clear.

"OOD, any idea what that might be?"

"Looks like a huge static charge, however, the Geiger counters on the outside skin recorded a huge surge of radiation right before they lost power. The reading was 4025 milli-Sieverts where radiation treatment for cancer is 250 milli-Sieverts. This would kill you quickly. It was still there after everything came back now dropping since we are about out of the field.".

"Conn, Sonar."

"Sonar, go ahead?"

"Sir, we have just passed through the radiation energy field we were detecting. It is clear in front of us.".

"Sonar, Aye."

The COB said, "Captain! Sir, our speed has dropped to zero. Should we try to apply power again?".

"OOD, accelerate to 18 knots".

"Aye Sir."

"Captain, it's working we are accelerating on course 2-2-0.".

"OOD, hold course and speed."

"OOD, Aye.

"Radar, Conn."

"Radar, Aye."

"Radar, do you have anything on your screen?"

"Sir, we are getting a trace back where we went through the energy field. The Radar signal appears to bounce off the field, that and the Atoll itself is all. No ships or planes."

"Conn, Aye."

"Photonics, Conn."

"Photonics, Aye."

"Photonics can you see anything?"

"Sir, we have pulled far enough away that I can't see the blue field anymore. However, the Atoll looks different, things are a healthier green looking and there appear to be people on the far side of it."

"Conn, Aye"

On the PA, "All hands, this is the Captain. We have experienced some form of high energy radiation effect. Please make damage and injury reports to the OOD.".

"Conn, Radio."

"Radio, what do you have?"

"Sir, that's my problem, I have nothing!"

"Radio, what the heck do you mean?"

The Radioman on KANE is Petty Officer Billy George. He is 20 years old, husky blond. He has a history as a Ham radio operator and skilled computer hacker. He can fix almost anything electronic or computerized, just by instinct. He does an excellent job of running the ship's communication. This he couldn't fix!

"Captain, I have nothing on the normal satellite communication system, it can't even find the satellites when I ping them. The high-frequency system is also on but receiving nothing. The air is absolutely dead, I am receiving nothing at all. I can't even get the weather updates."

"Radio, keep me informed."

"Radio, Aye."

In the Radio Room, Lieutenant Williams walked over to try to help, "Petty Officer George, have you tried the Very Low-Frequency system?"

Petty Officer George threw some switches on the massive communication console. On the touch screen terminal in front of him, he tried to adjust the receivers and crank up the gain as much as possible.

"Lieutenant, I am getting some slow and very distant Morse code signals. Let me scan around and see what happens if I feed the code to the computer."

Then he started to get text displays which were the computer's translation of the characters being received in Morse code. The messages were very broken. The computer translated the Morse, but the resulting letters said nothing in English. Then the Petty Officer told the computer to try to translate this group of letters, thinking maybe it was Chinese. In a few minutes of searching, the computer found something, the only words the computer could make out were *Marine, landings, and Guadalcanal.* Most of the rest of the message was garbage.

Lieutenant Williams said, "Did you notice the cipher code used to translate that original message. It says it's a code from WWII in the Pacific?".

The Lieutenant thought for a minute and then said, "I need to get this to the Captain."

He grabbed the mike and said, "Conn, Como."

"Conn, Aye."

"Sir, we have found some interesting information I need to show you."

"Lieutenant, I am calling a meeting in the Wardroom, bring it with you."

The Captain announced, "All officers to the Wardroom, now!".

The Wardroom is a fairly small room where the officers eat their meals and have meetings. It has a long narrow table that will seat ten and the Captain and the XO sit at the heads of the table.

The Captain walked into the Wardroom did a quick mental attendance check. He saw all his officers where there:

- XO- Lieutenant Commander Michael Mascoll

- Communications -Lieutenant Martin Williams

- Weapons- Lieutenant Commander William North

- Navigation-Lieutenant Malcolm Smithy

- Engineering-Lieutenant Commander Scotty Brown

- Assistant Engineering Officer, Lieutenant Paulo Rodrigues

The Captain started, "Gentlemen, I want your reports on where things stand?"

Lieutenant Williams spoke first, "Captain, communication is working fine as far as we can tell. There is not very much to hear and no one can hear us. Petty Officer George has found that we have an almost complete communication failure. Nothing is wrong with our equipment, there is just nothing to hear. He can't even find the satellites. He was able to find a message in Morse code on the Very Low-Frequency receiver. When he had the computer translate the code, it came up with letters that didn't say anything in English. He asked the computer to search for a translation. It found a cipher code that was used in WWII.

The end result is the computer translated the message and the only readable part was the three words, *Marine, landings,* and *Guadalcanal.* He also said that the frequency he received was used in WWII and it was very weak. Apparently, the transmission we received is what they call, 'Skip'. Kind of a radio signal bouncing around between earth and space traveling the globe. I don't know what that tells us?"

The Captain said, "Lieutenant, I guess a call to Pacific Submarine Fleet Command is not going to happen?"

"No Sir, that is pretty much out at this time."

34

Then the next to speak was Lieutenant Commander Brown, the head of Engineering. He said, first a little housekeeping report. The reactor, turbine generators, and propulsor drive are all functioning normally. They took a bit of a hit going through that field, but everything came right back. As for what happened, I don't have a clue."

Then the XO, Lieutenant Commander Mascoll spoke, "Sir, Photonics is no longer able to see the wall of the energy field since we have moved away. Radar reported they have nothing on the ocean or in the sky. They would normally be seeing at least planes. Sonar is reporting some whales close to the Atoll which really would not normally happen. That is about all I have.".

The Captain looked at his watch and said, "This is August 5th. Let me think about this a second...In the year 1942, in two days the Marines would stage a major amphibious landing on the island of Guadalcanal. Could this possibly mean we are receiving a message transmitted during WWII?"

Commander Williams said, "Sir, that seems to be somewhat supported by the evidence between the frequency we are receiving the message on, the low signal strength and the fact that the transmission seems to be talking about the landing at Guadalcanal. Sir, I think of two possible plans.

First, we could head to Pearl Harbor and try to contact the command at this time. The second idea, we could head for Guadalcanal close to the battle we suspect is happening, to make contact with the Allied Fleet there.".

Commander North was getting a bit excited and jumped into the conversation kind of loudly, "What in the hell would a boat with the weapons we carry do in a WWII battle! One nuke and we could remove the whole fleet. How do we fight in that kind of battle? This is nothing we have ever experienced."

The XO spoke up, "Commander North, calm down. We can use our torpedoes and maybe other ordinance the same way we always would just at a weaker target. Don't let the situation get to you, we are all thinking the same things.".

"Aye Sir"

The XO continued, "Captain, I think I support William's second idea. Head toward Guadalcanal and try to get orders from command there, whoever that may be. If it is 1942, it is too late to do anything to help at Pearl Harbor, might as well be where the action is."

The Captain asked, "Anything else men?" He paused for a few seconds looking around the table.

"Alright if you don't have anything else, I am going to agree and say that our plan will be to head to what we think is WWII in the Pacific Theater and go from there. Everyone alright with that?"

All the officers together said, "Aye, Captain."

"So that is our plan. I am going to head for Guadalcanal. See to your departments, keep your men ready and informed. Thanks. You're dismissed."

They all rose to go back to their stations.

NEW ORDERS

August 5, 2025, Time 10:22, Near the Bikini Atoll
in the Pacific Heading for Guadalcanal

Captain Richey ran back to the Conn. The announcement was made, "Captain has the Conn.".

He grabbed the microphone and said, "All Hands, this is the Captain. As you all know, we experienced an unexplained area of very high radioactive energy as we passed near Bikini Atoll. We have no idea what caused it and can only speculate it has something to do with the heavy atomic bomb testing done there. We have communication only by code on a Very Low-Frequency system, but Petty Officer George was able to decode a mysterious message that appears to be from the command of forces during WWII in the Pacific. I am not able to contact COMSUBPAC, so apparently, right now we have no chain of command.

If you know your history, you will know that on August 7, 1942, in two days, the U.S. Marines will conduct a major amphibious landing at a well know place called Guadalcanal. According to the broken message, the Petty Officer translated the words; *Marine, landings, and Guadalcanal* came out.

We believe there is some possibility that the energy field somehow caused us to jump back in time to 1942. It makes me hear Twilight Zone music, believe me. I can't even begin to explain this.

I intend to sail closer to that battle area and attempt to contact the commander of the fleet and get some orders. That is all."

Then he said, "Navigator, plot an open ocean course to take us near Guadalcanal.".

"Captain course plotted. Recommend new course 1-8-5."

"Officer of the Deck, steer course 1-8-5, depth 350 feet, speed 25 knots.".

"Aye Captain!"

◆ ◆ ◆

The Captain said, "OOD I am going to my cabin to do some research.".

"Aye, Sir. OOD has the conn."

♦ ♦ ♦

The Captain walked back to his cabin to do some research in his library of naval history books. As he sat down, he saw the picture of his beautiful wife Jean hanging on the wall above his desk. He wondered if he would ever get back to her, in their time. He thought about his beautiful and historic 1942, Breitling Cronomat, Mariner's Chronograph. This watch was given to him as a present from his wife. She found it at a pawn shop, they had no real story on it except they were told it was in a ship sinking in WWII and found by hobby divers. It had been cleaned and reconditioned. Interestingly considering the current conditions, the watch had already been here once. But will it ever see 2025 again?

He has done a lot of reading about historical battles like Guadalcanal. He believes there is a lot to learn from those old battles. He tries to learn from the mistakes made by those commanders, now documented and analyzed in many books and articles.

Over time all kinds of naval historians dissect Naval actions and find every bad decision the command made and it is all there. It is so much easier, for them after the fact when they are writing the articles and they didn't have to make the decision. He now has a very unique advantage of being able to read the exact progression of the landing at Guadalcanal and the Battle of Savo Island.

He read on August 9th the USS Quincy; a New Orleans Class cruiser was sunk by the Japanese fleet in the very early stages of the Battle of Savo Island after it supported the landing on Guadalcanal.

He didn't know why but that particular incident really got to him. He didn't know anyone who had been on the Quincy or really anything about it. It just kind of hit a Big Brother note with him, telling him to go protect that little brother. The Captain decided that without further orders that just might be his first mission, to defend the Quincy in 1942. He would love to just call them on the radio and warn them what was coming. Enough so they could avoid the sneak attack by the Japanese. His better judgment told him not to discuss the time travel or advertise what his ship is, except to the command. Some believe anything like that could cause the sci-fi book time paradox. At this point, he was not at all sure what to believe.

Walking back to the control he was thinking, "For lack of anything else, I'll create my own orders to take out the two cruisers that attacked the USS Quincy, saving over 350 brave American sailors."

◆ ◆ ◆

The Captain walked back to the Conn and signaled the XO to come over and talk. The Captain said, "Mike in my research I have determined that we might be of more value in that battle if we stay out of the main landing effort. That was all very confused and fluid. My research says the Japanese 8th Fleet commanded by Vice Admiral Gunichi Mikasa, at this time would be at Rabaul. They will be attacking the Allied fleet near Savo Island from the north. They will ultimately sink or damage five Allied ships at that battle. I think we should change course to New Ireland try to contact the command of the Allied fleet. If we can't get them, then stop that Japanese Fleet, saving hundreds of Allied lives. What do you think about that theory?"

The XO said, "Captain, honestly this scares the crap out of me. You know the old sayings about having two little men on your shoulders each one giving you different instructions. One of mine says we should just stay out of histories' way. The other says we go and kick ass. I guess your idea sounds like as good a plan as any. If we are in 1942, that is a battle we can take on. Our experience and our Boat will give the Japanese fleets something to have nightmares about. Let's do it."

The Captain said, "Let me look at a few more things."

"Yes, Sir."

Then the Captain walked down to the navigation plot display and took a detailed look at where they were heading and the relationship between the Japanese Fleets location at Rabaul, Savo Island, and Guadalcanal. The plot display is a large video display with a touch screen and a lot of navigation tools in a massive menu down the side. Right now, without GPS, the navigator was having to manually plot their position. A swipe of the Captain's fingers on the computer touch screen opened the map up so he could see their approximate current position and Rabaul both on the screen. Then by touching the two locations, he could do a few calculations. Then he asked the Navigator Seaman James, "About 45 hours total if we went to New Ireland, right?"

"That looks about right, Sir."

Seaman James looked at the Captain and smiled saying,

"This is going to be interesting, Sir!".

"You can bet on that, James."

The Captain walked back to the Conn and they announced, "Captain has the Conn."

The Captain picked up the mike and said, "All officers on the communication net."

The Captain picked up a separate phone. It provided a conference call with all the various departments and their officers. The Captain said, "I have done some more research on the subject of the attack on Guadalcanal and the Battle of Savo Island. The XO and I believe that we can be of more value if we head for Rabaul. There is currently a Japanese fleet there and if this is 1942, they will play a big part in sinking or damaging five Allied ships at Savo Island. As soon as we are in that area, we will attempt to contact the command of our fleet and get definite orders. However, the XO and I agree that we head there away from the very fluid battles at Guadalcanal. Anyone have any input on that decision?".

Lieutenant Commander North a bit heatedly said, "Sir, I am not sure I totally agree. Our firepower in a battle like the main landing forces at Guadalcanal could easily cause more harm than good. But at Savo island, we have the same problem on a smaller scale."

No one said anything else so, the Captain closed in a bit of a frustrated tone, "Commander, I appreciate your input. However, we are changing our plan and heading for New Ireland.".

The Captain picked up the mike, "All Hands this is the Captain. We are still sailing without the guidance of Pacific Submarine Command. The only assumption we can go on at this point is that the energy field somehow caused us to jump back in time to 1942.

History tells us the Japanese 8th Fleet commanded by Vice Admiral Gunichi Mikasa, at this time would be at Rabaul. The Fleet consists of five heavy cruisers, two light cruisers, and a destroyer. That fleet will engage the Allies at Savo Island on August 8, 1942.

That battle was given the nickname of **The Battle of Five Sitting Ducks**. That refers to the allied losses from the swift attack by Admiral Mikasa's fleet.

If this assumption proves to be true, we may now be involved in WWII in the Pacific Theater.

I intend to sail close to New Ireland and that battle area and attempt to contact the commander of our fleet and get some orders. If we cannot make contact, we will attack that fleet. That is all."

Then he said, "Navigator, plot an open ocean course to take us near the southern tip of New Ireland.".

"Captain recommend course 2-2-5."

"Officer of the Deck, steer course 2-2-5, depth 350 feet, speed 25 knots.".

"Aye Captain!"

The Captain talking quietly to the XO, "Mike we have about 40 hours till we get in range to start evaluating the Japanese Task Force. I am a little concerned about North. We need to get the men rested and fed because there may be some long days coming. You want a break for a while?".

"Aye, Sir. North will be OK, just the unknown."

"Very Well. XO you are relieved."

SLIDING ACROSS THE PACIFIC

August 6, 2025, Time 14:22, in the Pacific

497 miles from New Ireland

The XO woke up in his bunk, actually surprised he slept well for about the last 4 hours. He cleaned up a bit and then walked to the Control Room.

The Captain and XO had switched off a couple of times as the big boat slid along 350 feet under the Pacific for some 28 hours. The announcement was, "XO in the Conn!".

Just then the Captain checked, "Officer of the Deck, what is our current status?".

"Captain, we are currently 497 miles from New Ireland. the course is now 2-6-0, depth 350 feet, speed 25 knots. Everything is functioning normally.".

"XO, have you set up a short 3-hour shift rotation to get the men all fed and some sack time?"

"Yes, Sir. They are getting some rest. We are still about 14 hours from New Ireland so they will all be cycled through rest period by then."

The Captain said quietly to the OOD, "Come over here."

They walked away from the activity of the Control Room so the Captain could talk to him. "Lieutenant, this is going to be a totally new form of operation for all of us. We actually know in advance where the enemy will be, when, and what their plan is. I am a bit concerned that all of that will be a lot to manage along with the operation of the ship and weapons. I want you to pick a Senior Enlisted man to act as a kind of Statistician. If you can find someone who loves history it would be great. Their job will be to keep us informed about how we are, let's say interfacing, with the historic war.".

"Captain, I have just the man, Chief Petty Officer McClennan. He loves the history of WWII and as you know he is a navigator and has the chart skills."

"Sounds good Lieutenant, relieve him of normal duty and explain what we are going to want from him. Assign him to do battle research using the library in my cabin. Thanks, Lieutenant.".

The Captain walked back up to the main command area. Then he gave an unusual command. "Radio, Conn."

"Conn, Radio Aye."

"Radio, we are about 497 miles from New Ireland. I know the radio systems in 1942 were not very powerful, but our receivers are. I am going to pop-up and run at periscope depth for about a half-hour, so we can raise the masts. I want you to see if you can hear anything from the Guadalcanal area, Japanese or Allied."

"Radio, Aye Captain."

"OOD, at the same time I want the Photonics and Radar activated to see on long-range if there is anything near us."

"Aye, Captain".

The OOD commanded, "COB, Slowly, make your depth 90 feet, let the men sleep, raise the masts."

◆ ◆ ◆

In a few minutes, the masts of the USS Joseph Kane broke the surface again into a bright, clear, very hot, August day. The Radio, Radar, and the Photonics Masts were all being used to reach out across the waves for current information. Well, maybe 1942 current information.

The OOD said, "Captain, we are down to 15 knots with the drag of the masts and this close to the surface, recommend we break this off and submerge again.".

"You are absolutely right Lieutenant".

The OOD said, "Lower the masts and continue on course, make our depth 350 feet, increase speed to 30 knots."

"Radio, Captain."

"Radio, Aye."

"Radio, what did you get?"

"Sir, as you know code transmission carries much further than voice. I got a little very broken voice communication, sounded like positioning reports about the Japanese near Bougainville, the computer translated the Japanese, but it was all talking in code words. I did get some code transmission. It again didn't make sense in normal Morse, so I ran it through the computer database. It found this time it was an encrypted code used by the Japanese in WWII. The computer translated it and it was a report from some floatplanes overflying the area to Vice-Admiral Mikasa, indicating that a large number of Amphibious Landing support ships are on the move near Guadalcanal. They acknowledged the message but had no orders or responses. That was it, Sir".

"Radio mark that code for reference, you will be hearing a lot more of it. Thanks."

"Photonics, anything visual?"

"Captain, the sun is just starting to come up to our port so our visibility was excellent. We saw nothing except one very old looking cargo ship under what appeared to be the Philippine flag. Nothing else in the area."

"Very well."

"Conn, Radar."

"Radar, go ahead."

"Sir, I have absolutely nothing. No ships or planes visible on my scope other than that one cargo ship."

"Conn,   Aye."

August 6, 1942, Time 22:22, in the Pacific

221 miles from New Ireland

The big flat black colored submarine has been speeding along under the Pacific for 8 hours since the radio check. The XO and Captain have switched off a couple of times trying to back up the OOD and keep alert. The Captain was just walking into the Control Room carrying a fresh cup of coffee he brought from the mess.

"Captain in the Conn."

There are two OODs to take shifts. The OOD on duty is Lieutenant Brodsky. He is about a ten-year submarine man working very hard for his own command.

The Captain noticed that the XO was involved in something at one of the stations so he said, "OOD, what is our current status?"

"Captain, we are 221 miles from New Ireland, depth 350 feet, speed 30 knots. The boat is fully operational.".

The XO walked back over and the Captain said, "XO you and the OOD are relieved to go get some chow. The steaks are out of sight tonight. Thank God for freezer space."

"Aye, Captain."

"I stand relieved."

"Captain has the Conn"

The Captain grabbed the mike, "Radio, this is the Captain."

"Radio, Aye."

"I want to try another quick run at periscope depth to take a clear listen. Turn on your recorders and be ready it is going to be short."

"Radio, Aye."

"Photonics, get a good look around while we are up there."

"Photonics, Aye."

"COB, make your depth 90 feet, raise the masts, maintain ahead full."

"Aye, Captain."

The masts again popped through the surface of the Pacific. This time the sun was starting to set in front of them to their starboard. The Photonics Masts' cameras have very sophisticated filters to shield the bright light so the view is normally acceptable even into the sun."

"Radio, what did you get?"

"Captain, I am picking up code transmissions both in encrypted Allied code and Japanese code. The action at Guadalcanal is getting ready to start at first light tomorrow. The amphibious support ships are in place. Admiral Trainer has ordered the cruisers, USS Quincy, USS Astoria, and USS Vincennes to a position north-east of Savo Island. The Radar Pickets USS Blue and USS Randolph Talbot have been ordered to surveillance patrols north-east and north-west of Savo Island. The Japanese Taskforce is being assembled."

"Very well."

"Photonics anything to see up there?"

"Captain, there was not much to see a couple very old design commercial ships moving around. Nothing of interest."

"Very well."

Just then the OOD walked back into the conn. The Captain said, "OOD you have the Conn; I will be in the Wardroom."

"Aye, Sir. OOD has the Conn."

◆ ◆ ◆

The Captain walked to the Wardroom grabbed a coffee and sat down with the XO. "XO, how is that steak?"

"Sir, it is wonderful. The more modern the boats get the better we live, I love it. I don't think they ate steak on the Diesel Boats."

"XO, how do you feel about our situation?"

"Captain, honestly very nervous. I don't like the idea of having no command chain. We are both experienced officers and I trust in our ability to make good decisions. As far as we know, no one has ever been in this situation, so we have nothing to go by. It now seems the assumption is right and we are in 1942. Heading for a battle with the Japanese. What is the impact of that?"

"Mike, I have no idea. I am hoping to be able to contact the commander of the Amphibious Fleet and get some orders. I know that would make me feel much better. However, they will not understand what we are and what we bring to the table. As you said, we both just need to utilize our experience."

"I agree, Captain."

"How is the crew doing?"

"Sir, they are all a bit nervous as we are, about what all this means. I had to break up a little fight in the passageway. Nothing big, just a lot of tension boiling over. I have asked the Supervisors to all keep their men informed about what we are doing and what is happening. It helps them to not feel like they are trapped in a can."

"Mike, I do remember that feeling from early in my career. If we could stop at a beach and spend a few hours it would fix us right up. Unfortunately, I don't think World War II is going to wait for us to chill out."

"Aye, Sir."

♦ ♦ ♦

A little more than 6 hours more with the big black bullet sliding silently through the Pacific. No hits on the Sonar, there is just nothing around, not even a whale. Then they arrive at the active area, that is the World War II active area.

NOW IT BEGINS

August 7, 1942, Time 04:22, in the Pacific

14 miles east of the southern tip of New Ireland

The XO had the conn on this shift so the Captain walked into the Radio Room and asked, "Petty Officer George, can our computer transmit using those codes you have been receiving?".

"Yes Sir, communication will be slow because of the human on the other end having to decode the message.".

The Captain grabbed the mike and said, "XO this is the Captain, make your depth 90 feet and raise the masts."

"Aye, Captain."

"Petty Officer George contact Admiral Trainer's ship the HMAS Australia."

It took four or five minutes but then an answer was received the computer displayed the decrypted message. They both watched the display as the message came back, "HMAS Australia, Sub-Lieutenant Anderson."

The Captain said, George, send, 'This is Captain Richey, CO of the USS Joseph Kane.'".

The return message in a few minutes said, "Sir, we don't have a USS Joseph Kane in the registry. We do have a USS Kane a Destroyer?".

Send: "Sub-Lieutenant, I need to communicate directly with Admiral Trainer." Delay

"Sir, for security may I have your serial number?".

Send: "My serial number is 9456322.". Delay

"Sir, I am sorry that does not show in my command book as a valid active Captain's serial number. I can't accept your message."

There was a pause for a minute during which Captain Richey's blood pressure must have been ringing the bell. After a deep breath, trying to be calm he continued.

Send: "Sub-Lieutenant, I am a Captain in the United States Navy. I am the CO of a Nuclear Attack submarine the USS Joseph Kane. Now, you connect me with the Admiral or I will guarantee you will be swabbing decks on every ship in the Allied fleet!".

After a very, very long pause, the message came back. "This is Rear Admiral Richard Trainer, Commander of the Pacific Amphibious Forces. The Sub-Lieutenant said there is a security issue. Something like your serial number, name and the name of your ship are not valid. Please explain Captain?".

Send: "Admiral, my name is Captain Walter Richey. Serial number 9456322. I am the CO of SSN-809, the USS Joseph Kane a Virginia Class Nuclear Attack Submarine. My boat went through a very strong radioactive energy field near Bikini Atoll and I need instructions?"

Another long delay then, "Captain, we don't have a Virginia Class Submarine. Our latest submarines are Gato Class, diesel-electric boats. I have no idea what a nuclear submarine is. Obviously, Captain, we have a couple of problems to work out.".

Send: "Yes, I would certainly agree with that, Sir!". Delay.

"Do you have any ideas, Captain?".

Send: "Sir, I just have one theory you will think is strange. What date is it?". Delay.

"What do you mean Captain, it is August 7, 1942.".

Send: "I can't explain why or how, but to me, my crew and all the equipment on board, it is August 7, 2025!". Delay.

"How could that be?"

Send: "Admiral, I have no idea. All I know is August 5th at about 09:10, near Bikini Atoll, my boat passed through a very high-level field of radiation energy which temporarily shut down all of our systems and scanned us with a blue wave. Since the nuclear bomb testing was done at Bikini Atoll. That may have been some residual radiation field underwater near those tests.".

Another very long delay, "Captain, what is all this talk about nuclear power and radiation testing at Bikini Atoll?".

Send: "I am sorry, Sir. That's right for you that hasn't happened yet. Are you aware of the Manhattan Project?"

Delaying again, "Captain, How the hell do you know about that. It is 'Eyes Only, Top Secret' information and it only started a couple of months ago?".

Even in Morse Code, you could hear how mad the Admiral was.

Send: "As I told you, Sir, to me it is history. You can read about it in hundreds of books.".

Another long delay, it was taking time to process these long messages on their end.

"Captain, for the security of the country, do not mention any of that again, to anyone, repeat anyone! Got it?".

Send: "Yes, Sir. I understand. What am I supposed to do now, Sir?". Delay.

"Is your boat fully operational now?".

Send: "Yes, sir all stations are reporting full operation."

Another delayed response, "Captain, I don't begin to know why I should even believe this story. I have never heard of time travel, a nuclear submarine or an of this. I have no idea what the capability of your boat is, but I think it is clear that it far exceeds our Gato Class submarines."

Send: "Yes Sir, by a factor of 1000."

The next one came pretty fast, it seemed like the Admiral was dictating responses before even completely reading the message, "Captain, I have a Top-Secret order for you."

There was a very long delay, most likely caused by both ends chewing on this long message. Then the computer started typing on the display slowly as it was still translating the message as it went along, "We have a plan for a massive amphibious landing by the Marines on the island of

Guadalcanal and Tulagi today August 7th at first light. We believe that the Imperial Japanese Navy's, new 8th Fleet will be dispatched to disrupt that landing. Vice Admiral Gunichi Mikasa currently has that fleet at Rabaul and as far as we know they have not begun to move to the Guadalcanal area. We believe the Fleet consists of one heavy cruiser, two light cruisers, and a destroyer. Your orders will be to attack that Japanese Fleet and use any means you have to do it.

If you are willing to attack the Japanese, I have to at least believe you are on our side. Whatever kind of boat you are commanding."

Send: "Sir with all due respect, believe me when I tell you that is a lot of power. Are you sure, Sir?".

Another long pause, "Yes Captain, I am sure. Just be sure you are shooting at Japanese ships or we will have to try to take you out. I will send private messages to our fleet captains that there is a new boat in operation in the area. I will send you the critical radio frequencies to talk or communicate to our fleet, ship to ship, or code. I will tell them you have the code name 'Scorpion'."

Send: "I understand the orders, Admiral, and we are currently 14 miles from New Ireland and heading that way."

They quickly responded, "Good hunting, Captain!"

Send: "Thank you, Sir! Out."

"Petty Officer George, that was painful but well done. I can't believe what we have been thrown into."

"Me neither, Sir,"

♦ ♦ ♦

The Captain walked back into the Control Room.

"Captain has the Conn.".

The Captain grabbed the mike and announced, "All Hands this is the Captain. We have succeeded in communicating with Rear Admiral Richard Trainer, Commander of the Pacific Amphibious Forces, and in command of the landing at Guadalcanal. We have confirmed that we indeed have transported ourselves to 1942 in the middle of WWII in the Pacific Theater.

The Admiral has ordered us to attack the Japanese Fleet which will be leaving Rabaul and we know it will attack the Allied ships at Savo Island. He has said for us to use all our facilities to complete this order. I tried to explain how much power that is but frankly, he has no idea.

Now like everyone in the Navy, I just take orders even in 1942. We could have a huge debate about the pros and cons of this order. We may also rightfully worry about the impact on us in the future, in our time. If we see our time again? We have no information to even evaluate that. Even in the year 2025, no one knows the impact of time travel. Do your jobs and don't spend all your time worrying, we just don't know.

All I can say is that as of tomorrow there will be a big change in history as the power of the USS Joseph Kane is displayed to the 1942 Japanese Navy. That is all.".

The whole crew cheered in support of the Captain, their team, and boat.

◆ ◆ ◆

In a few minutes, the Captain, XO, and the OOD were all in the Control Room. It was getting close to the time for the first look at the action in 1942. There was a wave of tension in the room, but everyone was ready.

The Captain said, "OOD status please?".

"Captain, we are 14 miles east of New Ireland, course 2-0-0, depth is 150 feet, as ordered by the XO we have reduced speed to 5 knots."

"Very well."

"OOD bring Chief Petty Officer McClennan to the Conn and meet me in Navigation. XO, I would like you there too we should be OK for a few minutes."

In Navigation a couple of minutes later the Captain began to explain, "Chief Petty Officer McClennan, I believe the Lieutenant has described to you what we want you to do. We have the astounding advantage of knowing exactly how this battle was supposed to go and how the Japanese will be moving. We need to track our operations against that history so we have an idea of how we can best prevent their movement and then step on to the next position. Feel free to speak up and let us know where there are opportunities or problems.".

The Petty Officer said, "Aye, Sir.".

The Captain continued pointing to the navigation screen. When he touched a menu and a location, a Waypoint marked Point 'B' was added to the screen about 10 miles east of Bougainville at Kieta. He said, "If I recall properly the

Japanese Task Force will be moving by here tonight, Aug 7th at 16:22 heading for Kieta.".

The Petty Officer said, "That is my estimate too, Sir."

The Captain continued with his plan, "I want us to take a position here.". Pointing to a position just east of Green Islands, 32 miles north-east of where the Japanese Fleet will cross on their route to Kieta, this will be Waypoint 'A'. A distance of another 160 miles to my Waypoint 'B'. I think our Sonar will be able to track their cruisers as the cross in front of us, a Fleet makes a lot of noise. Once we get a fix on them turning south-east, we will slowly and quietly move in, off to their east, and then turn west and deliver some special new navy torpedoes. Everyone has to keep up because things will be changing quickly. After the first strike, we are rewriting history. Everyone OK with the initial plan?".

They all answered, "Aye, Sir".

"Ok, return to your stations. Chief Petty Officer, you can go to my cabin. I have naval history books, a computer terminal, and a printer. The only thing you can access is the ship's computer database but it has some good naval history too. Take a communication headset to talk to the OOD.".

"Aye, Sir."

The OOD said, "Navigator plot course to Point A."

"OOD, recommend course 1-8-5. Distance 60 miles"

"COB, make your course 1-8-5, speed 5 knots, depth 150 feet."

"Aye, Sir."

August 7, 1942, Time 7:50, 54 miles north-west of

Buka

Waypoint Marked Point A

After almost four hours more of sliding quietly through the Pacific toward the Battle of Savo Island, Captain Richey is walking to the Control Room thinking, "I am coming to a 1942 WWII Pacific battle bringing one of the most lethal Navy vessels ever devised, even in 2025. The Japanese Navy does not even have sonar to hear us coming. The Mark 48 Torpedoes we carry have a range of 38 Km (24 miles) at 55 knots (about 63 mph), using its own internal guidance. We will be taking advantage of that by firing at a range where the Japanese will not even know where it came from until it is far too late. I sure wish I could call my wife Jean and tell her this story. I certainly hope I get the chance to at least see her again. Hey Richey, get back to work.".

The Captain walked into the Control Room, "Captain has the Conn."

"Officer of the Deck status please?"

"Captain, we have just arrived at Waypoint A and are patrolling the area at a depth of 150 feet.".

"Very well."

"Conn Sonar."

"Sonar Aye."

"What do you have?"

"Captain, I have some ship noise in the water but nothing close enough to identify."

"Very Well."

"Conn Radio."

"Radio Aye."

"Radio I am going to do another run at periscope depth so you can check on radio traffic."

"Radar take a look on the distant range; Photonics be ready to get a look around with your night scopes."

"OOD, make your depth 90 feet and raise the masts."

The pilot steered the boat slowly up to 90 feet and the masts broke the surface.

"Photonics, anything close?"

"No Sir, we can just barely see their cross over point and there is no ocean traffic.".

"Radio Conn, "What did you get?".

"Captain, there is a lot of radio traffic on both sides. The landing at Guadalcanal is well underway. The Allied patrol ships have been notified of the progress. On the Japanese side, Vice-Admiral Gunichi Mikasa has boarded his Flagship the heavy cruiser Chokai. The Japanese Task Force near Rabaul was then ordered to prepare to sail their destination about 10 miles east of Bougainville.

I have a good one for you, Sir, I received a message from the USS S-38 a submarine they call an S Boat. The computer doesn't have any more information on it. They radioed in that they spotted the Japanese Taskforce in St. George Channel, leaving Rabaul. She was too close to fire torpedoes and almost got hit by the lead ship. That is about it right now sir, I will review the tapes and see if there is anything else."

"Very well."

Radar, Conn."

"Radar, Aye."

"Radar, did you see anything?"

"Sir, nothing close enough to identify."

"Conn, Aye."

"OOD, retract the masts and make your depth 150 feet again, recommence patrolling the area."

"Aye Captain."

The Captain said privately to the OOD, "Well we will make up for S-38's miss. Anyway, what the heck is an S-Boat? Oh, never mind."

"Captain, Navigator."

"Captain Aye, what do you have?"

"Sir, I just wanted to confirm that the coordinates I got on the Japanese orders, from the radio room are almost exactly where you marked Waypoint B."

"Thanks, it's not magic, but it does help to know in advance."

"Aye, Sir."

The Captain picked up the mike and announced, "All hands, this is the Captain. We are in the position I have selected for our first attack on the 1942 Imperial Japanese Navy. We have that great luxury of knowing exactly when they will move and where. The Japanese Taskforce has begun to leave Rabaul for a position about 32 miles south of our current position where they will turn south-east. They will end up stopping East of Bougainville, the city of Kieta some 190 miles south-east. In other words, they are coming right by us. We intend to pick them up as they come by and trail them.

History says they will stop at that position fearing daytime attack from the carrier forces at Guadalcanal. They will arrive at that holding point tomorrow, August 8th at about 09:00. They will stay there for 6 hours to time their approach to Savo Island for the evening sunset, trying to avoid those air attacks. I estimate our first action on August 8th at 11:00. We will continue with the rest rotations the XO has set up till about 09:00 tomorrow. Get some rest and chow when you can. Those on watch make sure your station is completely ready for battle. I am not going to order Ultra Quiet, but keep the noise to a minimum. Carry on men.".

"XO you have the Conn."

"Aye, Sir XO has the Conn."

August 7, 1942, Time 22:30, 32miles north-east of

the Japanese track north of Bougainville

Waypoint Marked Position A

After a short rest and a couple of cups of Navy coffee, the Captain walked back into the Control Room.

"Captain has the Conn".

"OOD, you are relieved, go take a little break."

"Aye, Captain"

By the Captain's plan and history, the Japanese Fleet should be just about to cross in front of them in about an hour, on their way to Kieta.

The Captain grabbed the mike and announced, "All hands this is the Captain. Men this is it, we are going to start tracking the Japanese task force as they move to their position east of Bougainville. They should reach that final position in 10 hours and 30 minutes at 09:00. Then they will sit there for six hours. The battle of Savo Island was nicknamed **'The Battle of Five Sitting Ducks'**. Well, I believe it is going to be able to keep the nickname in our version of history, it will just be different ducks! That is all."

"OOD, man battle stations!"

Again, the very loud claxon rang throughout the boat and the OOD announced, "All hands man battle stations. This is not a drill, repeat this is not a drill!".

The crew knew exactly where they were to be and got there fast.

"Sonar, Conn."

"Sonar, Aye."

"Do you have any tracks on the Japanese task force yet?"

"Yes Captain, it is a long distance but right now it appears that they have picked up another part of the fleet. I can hear more signatures faintly. I believe, with the help of the Statistician, it is coming down from Kavieng. We believe we are tracking five heavy cruisers and two light cruisers and what appears to be a destroyer. The destroyer is at the rear of the line they must be expecting to be hit from behind. They are currently 5 miles north-north-west from Buka Island. They are turning to a course about 1-3-0 and doing about 15 knots. I don't have sonar signatures yet so I can't, give you the names. However, the Statistician says they should be in order the heavy cruiser Chokai, heavy cruiser Aoba, heavy cruiser Kako, heavy cruiser Kinugasa, heavy cruiser Furutaka, light cruisers Tenryu and Yubari and the destroyer Yunagi. I have just gotten enough to build some computer sonar signatures for them all, and named them based on that history.".

"Sonar, Aye."

"Alright, Officer of the Deck, make your depth 90 feet, raise the masts."

"Radio, let me know what is going on."

"Photonics and Radar, see if you can get a fix on the fleet."

After the masts break the surface the investigation begins. In a few minutes, the Captain gets the reports.

"Conn, Radio."

"Radio, go ahead."

"Captain, I am receiving coded Japanese communication from Admiral Mikasa to the Fleet. His orders are for them to stop east of Kieta until further notice. The Fleet ships all acknowledged that order."

"Conn, Photonics."

"Photonics, what do you see?"

"Captain, we can just barely see the Fleet's searchlights on high range light amplifier but they are still 32 miles away and moving away from us on a course that appears to be still about 1-3-0. Their speed is slowing to about 10 knots. It looks like, they are still in the same order with the Destroyer last."

"Conn, Aye."

"Conn, Radar."

"Conn, Aye, what do you have?"

"Conn, I have a pretty good track on the fleet noise and confirm what Photonics said."

"Very well."

◆ ◆ ◆

The Captain handed the XO a handwritten note and ordered, "XO have Radio send this message using the Allied code to Admiral Richard K. Trainer, aboard the HMAS Australia."

Here was the message:

"To: Admiral Richard K. Trainer, HMAS Australia

> *SCORPION is on station just east of Green Island. We are observing a Japanese Fleet consisting of the heavy cruiser Chokai, heavy cruiser Aoba, heavy cruiser Kako, heavy cruiser Kinugasa, heavy cruiser Furutaka, light cruisers Tenryu and Yubari and the destroyer Yunagi. They are located north-east of Bougainville moving east of Kieta and are stopping with orders to hold there. We are about to take **decisive** action.*
>
> *Captain of Scorpion."*

"Navigator, plot a course to take us about 5 miles east of the Japanese Fleet."

"Captain, recommend course 1-0-0."

"OOD, steer course 1-0-0, speed 25 knots, make your depth 150 feet. Load torpedo tubes 1 and 2. Do not open the outer doors."

"Aye Captain."

The 377-foot-long, 7,900 metric ton submarine for the next 6 hours and 30 minutes, slipped very silently to catch up to the Japanese Fleet and pull up beside them on the east. At a range of 5 miles, they had no way to know the boat was pulling up there.

◆ ◆ ◆

"Conn, Sonar."

"Sonar, go ahead."

"Captain, the engines in the Fleet ships have stopped."

"Sonar, Aye."

"OOD, status please?"

"Captain, we are on course 1-0-0, speed 25 knots, tubes 1 and 2 are loaded and ready, outer doors are still closed, current location 5.5 miles east of the Japanese fleet who are stopped at Kieta."

"OOD, slow to 5 knots, make your depth 90 feet and raise the masts."

"Aye, Captain"

The big boat slowly came close to the surface and the masts punched into what was now morning sunlight.

"Conn, Photonics."

"Captain, we are slightly behind the destroyer and at a range of 5.2 miles east of it. Recommend course 1-9-5 to the Yanagi."

"OOD, steer course 1-9-5, maintain speed at 5 knots, open outer doors. Set the fish in tube 1 for automatic sonar location and give it the Destroyer's coordinates, set its speed to 50 knots, range 7 miles."

A whirlwind of activity was happening in the Control Room as the boat was prepared to fire a very real 2025 torpedo at the 1942 Japanese Navy. The Weapons Panel now flashed green lights.

The OOD said, "Torpedo tube 1 is ready, course 1-9-5, Photonics and Sonar confirm the target bearing and range."

The Captain yelled, "FIRE One!"

The Mark 48 Torpedo blew out of the tube and accelerated on a course directly at the Japanese Destroyer Yunagi. In less than a minute the destroyer must have somehow recognized the torpedo chasing them. They launched two depth charges off their port side. Luckily, they didn't have near the range needed and most likely didn't know what they were shooting at. They exploded almost a half-mile ahead of KANE. The whole ship could feel the two explosions, but no damage. It did serve to thicken the tension.

The XO was on his way back to Control. After hearing the torpedo, he was thinking, "The torpedo we use, is what is called an Advanced Capability (ADCAP) weapon. This is a 21-inch in diameter, 19-foot-long, a 3,520-pound package of death on its way to a ship that will have no idea it is coming till it's way too late."

The Captain said, "Sonar, status on the fish?"

"Captain, the torpedo is running hot, straight and normal, speed 51 knots, time to target 5 minutes, 26 seconds."

"Photonics, give me a bearing to the Chokai."

"Captain, recommend course 1-8-1."

The Captain said, "ODD, steer course 1-8-1, make your speed 5 knots, reload tube 1."

"Aye, Sir."

"Captain, the course is 1-8-1, speed 5 knots."

"Photonics, bearing and range to the Chokai?"

"Captain, recommend bearing 1-8-1, range 6.3 miles."

"OOD, set torpedo 2 for automatic sonar location and give it the Chokai's coordinates, set its speed to 50 knots, range 7 miles."

"Aye, Sir".

"Captain, the torpedo is ready. Photonics and sonar confirm bearing and distance."

The Captain then yelled, "FIRE Two!".

As another torpedo blasted out of the tube and quickly accelerated on its way to execute the heavy cruiser Chokai, the flagship of the Japanese Fleet. The Captain quietly told the OOD, "A present for Vice Admiral Mikasa."

The Captain said, "Sonar, status on both of the fish?"

"Captain, torpedo 1 is running hot, straight and normal, speed 51 knots, time to target 4 minutes, 6 seconds.

Torpedo 2 is running hot, straight and normal, speed 50 knots. Time to target 5 minutes, 40 seconds."

The Captain said, "OOD, have Photonics turn on the video recorders, this will be quite a show even at this distance."

"Aye, Captain."

The Captain, XO, and OOD all walked over to the control area LED displays being fed from the Photonics Masts.

The Captain said out loud, "Well Emperor, here is a gift from the New US Navy."

♦ ♦ ♦

The suspense was thick in the control room like a London fog. You could feel it seeping out of every man. This was a new world no one had been trained for. The crew was all doing their jobs the way they had been trained. But, all of them feared the whole situation.

The XO was watching this all happen and thinking, "Every member of the crew knows that they are about to change history. Everyone who likes Sci-Fi has read about the impact of a paradox caused by time travelers changing history. The situation talking about what happens if your father was a sailor on the USS Quincy and like over 300 heroes went down with that ship on this day in 1942. Today, this submarine is making it very possible that he would have survived. What changes and what are the impacts. The battle is obviously going to change the flow recorded in history and no one will know the results. If the crew of this submarine can't get back to their own time that is another group of paradoxical impacts. Good or bad, these are the Navy's orders and Captain Richey is executing them."

After 6 minutes of welling tension, the first torpedo hit the Japanese Destroyer Yunagi.

"Conn, Photonics."

"Conn, Aye."

"Captain, I am sure you have seen it but the first torpedo hit the Yunagi almost a mid-ship. There was a major explosion most likely an ammunition storage area, directly under her guns. The ship is on fire and both the bow and the stern are rising in the air. I think we broke her back."

There was a cheer from the Control Room crew. The Captain a little impatient yelled, "Quiet!". Two minutes later torpedo 2 struck the Chokai.

"Conn, Photonics."

"Conn, Aye."

"Captain, torpedo 2 hit the Chokai a bit toward the stern. There are some fires and the ship is quickly listing to port and going down at the stern. Still afloat but not well at all.".

"Conn, Sonar."

"Go ahead."

"Captain, I can hear the Destroyer breaking up. I think it will go down in minutes."

"OOD, have the Photonics display put on all video screens."

"Aye, Captain"

The Captain grabbed the mike, "All Hands, we have made the first strike. We have sunk the Destroyer Yunagi and seriously wounded their Flag Ship the heavy cruiser Chokai. This is a good start but there is a lot of this battle left. Leave the celebration till it is over. Keep on top of your job. Captain out!"

"Conn, Sonar."

"Go ahead Sonar."

"Captain, the Yunagi has now sunk. The Chokai is making some loud cracking sounds but still afloat, definitely taking water fast. The rest of the fleet has fired up their engines and headed on a course about 1-7-5 and coming to about 23 knots.".

"OOD verify with the Statistician that they would be heading toward the Slot at this point."

"Captain the report is that this is the way they would have gone, but they are now 5 hours early. They are traveling in bright daylight and will be easy for the US ships and planes to spot."

84

"Conn, Sonar."

"Sonar, Aye."

"Sonar, who is last in the line now?"

"Sir, it is the light cruiser Yubari. Range 9.4 miles and opening. Course 1-7-5."

"OOD, Close the tube doors, retract the masts, steer course 1-8-0, make your depth 400 feet, ahead flank, reload tubes 1 and 2."

"Aye, Captain."

"Sonar, Conn."

"Sonar, Aye."

"Sonar, let me know as soon as you can get a shooting solution on the Yubari."

"Aye, Captain."

The big boat took off like a rabbit chasing the hounds. The Captain was thinking, "If I can get close enough to get off one more shot, then run down to the Manning Strait and intercept the rest of them."

KANE was running about 9 miles an hour faster than the fleet. In five minutes, they had closed to a range of 7.2 miles.

The Captain looked at his watch and said, "Officer of the Deck, what is our speed?"

"Captain, Speed is 31 knots."

"OOD, I thought so." Talking quietly the Captain said, "Lieutenant, didn't the specs say the maximum speed of this boat was 29 knots?"

"Sir, that was just for the public press releases. This Jet Propulsor drive is the best thing they ever put into a submarine, quiet and fast. It is an amazing machine isn't it?"

"Lieutenant, I certainly agree with that. Very well."

"Sonar, Conn."

"Sonar, Aye"

"Bearing and range to the Yubari?"

"Captain, bearing 2-0-1, range 7.1 miles, closing fast."

"OOD, Open the outer doors, reduce speed to 10 knots. I want to take a sonar only shot at the Yubari. I am not going to risk the masts at this point. Let me know when the computer has a shooting solution.".

"In seconds the OOD announced, "Captain, shooting solution locked in, tube 1 is ready."

The Captain yelled, "Fire one!"

The torpedo took off to find its own way to the Japanese cruiser Yubari.

In two minutes, the Captain said, "Sonar, status of the fish?"

"Sir, the torpedo is running hot, straight and normal, the torpedo is active, tracking has locked onto the Yubari, speed 55 knots, range to target 2 miles."

Another suspenseful feeling washed over the control room. The torpedo was on its way, out of everyone's control doing its own thing.

A little under 2 minutes later, "Conn, Sonar."

"Sonar, Aye."

"Captain, the torpedo has hit the Yubari. I can hear multiple explosions and their propeller noise stopped immediately. I think we hit them dead astern."

"Conn, Aye."

The Captain looked at his small version of the navigation screen, then he ordered, "Navigator, plot a high-speed course to take us just north-west of Santa Isabel Island through the Manning Strait."

"Captain, recommend course 1-3-5, distance 156 miles."

Conn, Aye. Navigator, notify the OOD when we need to begin a turn to go through that strait."

"Navigator, Aye."

"OOD, Close outer doors, steer course 1-3-5, speed flank, depth 150 feet. Reload tube 1."

"Aye, Captain."

Trying to keep this a bit private, the Captain handed the XO another handwritten note and ordered, "XO have Radio send this message using the Allied code. Do you agree?"

He quickly read it and said, "Aye. Captain."

Here was the message:

"To: Admiral Richard K. Trainer, HMAS Australia

> *SCORPION is now just east of Keita. We have sunk the Destroyer Yunagi, critically wounded the Flagship the heavy cruiser Chokai and the light cruiser Yubari. We are observing the remainder of the Japanese fleet consisting of the heavy cruisers Aoba, Kako, Kinugasa, Furutaka, and the light cruiser Tenryu who are heading into the Slot at high speed. We will pursue but I am taking an alternate route. If the situation allows, we will attack them from Manning Strait.*
>
> *Captain of Scorpion."*

"OOD check what ships were the radar sentry ships guarding north of Savo Island?"

"Captain, the Statistician reports they were the destroyers USS Blue (DD-387) on the north-west and USS Ralph Talbot (DD-390) on the north-east."

"Very Well."

The Captain wrote another quick message, he handed the note to the XO and said, "Have radio send this to the Captains of the USS Blue (DD 387) and USS Ralph Talbot (DD-390).".

Here was this message:

"To: Captain USS Blue (DD 387) and Captain USS Ralph Talbot (DD-390)

SCORPION is now just east of Keita. We have sunk the Destroyer Yunagi, critically wounded the Flagship the heavy cruiser Chokai and the light cruiser Yubari. We are observing the remainder of a Japanese fleet consisting of the heavy cruisers Aoba, Kako, Kinugasa, Furutaka, and the light cruiser Tenryu who are heading into the Slot at high speed. We will pursue but we are taking an alternate route. If the situation allows, we will attack them from Manning Strait.

Captain of Scorpion."

The Captain calculated that they should be approaching the Slot and ready to go through the Manning Strait to cut off the Japanese fleet in about 4 hours and 20 minutes. He set the reminder on his watch.

ACTION IN 'THE SLOT'

August 8, 1942, Time 16:03 5 miles north-west of

Santa Isabel Island

Approaching 'The Slot'

KANE made a high-speed run in the more open Pacific to intercept the rest of the Japanese Fleet as they came down The Slot. The nickname "The Slot" was what they called the New Georgia Sound, the main waterway involved in merchant transit to and in the Solomon Islands. This waterway was very involved in the battle of Savo Island and Guadalcanal.

"Conn, Navigator."

"Navigator, go ahead."

"Captain, we are 5 miles from Manning Strait."

"Recommend course 1-8-9."

"Conn, Aye."

"Sonar, anything close?"

"No Sir, the closest ships are a distant ping almost 10 miles away, I believe they are heading south-east through the Slot."

"Conn, Aye."

"OOD, steer course 1-8-9, speed 20 knots, assume periscope depth and raise the masts. Radio and Photonics, I want the quick drill again. You have ten minutes."

The big boat steers up for a slow rise to 90 feet. Then the masts punch through the surface.

"Conn, Photonics."

"Photonics, go ahead."

"Sir, there is nothing close. I can see the traffic crossing Manning Straight traveling in the Slot. I can't really identify it."

"Conn, Radio."

"Go ahead."

"Captain, I just intercepted a coded message from the Japanese heavy cruiser Aoba. They were reporting to their new commander the sinking of both the Destroyer Yunagi, the light cruiser Yubari, and the heavy cruiser and flag ship

Chokai. They reported position 15 miles north-west of Santa Isabel Island in the Slot."

"Radio, Aye."

"Navigator, how far are we from entering The Slot?"

"Captain, we are about 8 miles to the center of New Georgia Sound."

"Navigator, what is our course through Manning Strait?"

"Captain, recommend course 1-8-9."

"OOD, steer course 1-8-9, speed 15 knots, retract the masts, and make your depth 100 feet."

"Aye, Sir."

The Captain was pushing some buttons on his really fancy chronometer watch. The boat was moving through Manning Strait to intercept The Slot at a 90-degree angle. Hopefully, they will get to the Sound, as the two Japanese cruisers get there coming down the slot.

♦ ♦ ♦

In one hour, his watch rang.

"OOD, slow to ahead 1/3, make your depth 90 feet, and raise the masts."

"Aye Sir."

"Masts raised, Sir."

"Photonics, can you see the Japanese Fleet coming down the slot?"

"Yes, Sir, I see part of it. The heavy cruisers Furutaka and Kinugasa are in line about 2 miles away moving on course 1-0-5. The light cruiser Tenryu is two miles behind them on the same course."

"Photonics, anything else close?"

"Sir, nothing I can see."

"Photonics, give me bearing and range to the Furutaka in the Channel."

"Conn, They are on bearing 2-2-4, range 4.5 miles."

"OOD, steer course 2-2-4, speed 2 knots. Make tubes 1 and 2 ready and open outer doors. Set the fish in tube 1 for automatic sonar location and give it the cruiser's coordinates, set its speed to 10 knots, range 5 miles."

Another surge of control activity as the torpedo was made ready to fire, then the green lights flash on.

"Conn, Sonar."

"Conn, Aye."

"The lead ship, Furutaka. is about to cross the opening at the mouth of the Manning Strait."

"Captain."

"Yes, OOD."

"Torpedo in tube 1 is ready, course 2-2-4, Photonics and Sonar confirm the target bearing and range."

The Captain yelled, "FIRE One!"

The big torpedo shot out of the tube and headed as a high-speed present addressed to the cruiser Furutaka.

"Conn, Sonar. Torpedo in the water! They must have gotten one shot off. Torpedo course 0-9-0, range 1 mile. This is going to be close!"

The Captain and the rest of the people in the Conn were all kind of internally panicked. They were all expecting an explosion. Listening to their heartbeats as the few seconds ticked by. The expected explosion didn't happen.

"Sonar, Conn."

"Sonar, Aye."

"Status of the Japanese torpedo?"

"Sir, I think our torpedo hit the ship just as they fired and it threw off their aim. It does not have tracking and it sounds like, their torpedo went on to the beach in front and to our port, but no explosion. I could hear its propeller screaming as it left the water."

"Photonics, report our torpedo's status."

"Captain, the Furutaka was hit just forward of midships. We must have hit some ammunition again because it blew in a big ball of fire. It is listing to Port and going down at the bow."

"Photonics, bearing and range to the Kinugasa."

"Captain, they are on bearing 2-2-7, range 3 miles. They have pulled past the Furutaka on her starboard. In two minutes, they have a clear side shot at us. If they know where we are."

"Sonar, how deep is the water here?"

"Sir, 295 feet in the channel."

"Navigator, plot a course south-east down the Sound."

"Captain, recommend course 1-5-5."

"OOD, close torpedo doors, retract the masts, steer course 1-5-5, ahead flank, make your depth 280 feet. Load tubes 5 and 6 and open the outer doors."

"Aye, Captain."

This is why they added rear torpedo tubes on this variant of the Virginia class submarines. The sailors in the aft torpedo room and the control area made those torpedoes ready to fire, the Weapons Control panel showed the green ready lights on tubes 5 and 6.

"Sonar, Conn."

"Sonar, Aye."

"Sonar, this is going to be your shot. Do you have a shooting solution for the Kinugasa?"

"Aye, Captain. Shooting solution is locked in."

The OOD said, "Captain. Torpedo in tube 5 is ready and locked on the solution."

The Captain yelled, "FIRE Five!"

The torpedo spat out the rear of KANE at the Japanese cruiser Kinugasa. Apparently in time before they could get a target on the sub after KANE moved so quickly and quietly."

"Conn Sonar, torpedo 5 running hot, straight and normal, course 2-8-5, range to target 150 yards.".

Two seconds and they felt a much smaller shock wave as the Kinugasa was hit.

"Sonar, report?"

"Sir, the Kinugasa was hit, sounds like in the bow, it is obviously taking water in the bow and has stopped. The cruiser Tenryu has apparently stopped to aid the Furutaka. I think they are going to have a tough time getting passed the two sinking cruisers anyway. They are both over 600 feet long, which is a pretty good blockade. One on each side of the channel according to my plot."

"Sonar, can you hear the other two Japanese cruisers in the slot?"

"No Captain, nothing moving down further in the Slot."

The Captain asked, "XO do you agree that the Aoba and Kako must have passed us and are further down the Slot?"

"Captain, I don't really know how they got down that fast, but Yes I have to agree."

"Sonar, how deep is the water here?"

"Sir, 295 feet at this point."

"Sonar best bearing south-east down the Sound."

"Captain, recommend course 1-5-5."

"OOD, close aft torpedo doors, retract the masts, steer course 1-5-5, make your speed 21 knots, depth 180 feet."

"Aye, Captain."

"Sonar, Captain."

"Sonar, Aye."

"Sonar keep a sharp listen as we move down the sound. We are not going to have the masts up so it's on you. I am going to push the speed up a bit to try to catch the rest of the Japanese Fleet. Report course changes directly to the Pilot."

"Aye, Captain."

"OOD, you oversee what is happening but I want Sonar to be able to call the shots to the Pilot. We are pushing the speed for a tight area like this, but I want to catch up to the rest of the Japanese Task Force.

"OOD, Aye."

♦ ♦ ♦

The Captain jotted down two notes, this message to the Captains of the Blue and the Ralph Talbot who are circling as Radar Pickets at the mouth of the entrance to Savo island:

> *"To: Captain USS Blue (DD 387) and Captain USS Ralph Talbot (DD-390)*
>
> *SCORPION has severely disabled cruisers Kinugasa and Furutaka, in the SLOT near Manning Strait. The cruiser Tenryu has stopped to lend assistance and is partially blocked from the channel. The rest of the Japanese Fleet must be further down the Slot. We are moving toward you to investigate.*
>
> *Captain of Scorpion."*

This same message to the Admiral:

> *"To: Admiral Richard K. Trainer, HMAS Australia*

> SCORPION has severely disabled cruisers Kinugasa and Furutaka, in the SLOT near Manning Strait. The cruiser Tenryu has stopped to lend assistance and is partially blocked from the channel. The rest of the Japanese Fleet must be further down the Slot. We are moving down the Sound to investigate.
>
> Captain of Scorpion."

The Captain handed his notes to the XO and said, "Have radio send these with the Allied code."

*August 8, 1942, Time 19:11, in the New Georgia
Sound, 65 miles north-west of Savo Island*

The mighty USS Joseph Kane has been sliding down the New Georgia Sound approaching the battleground for the naval battle of Savo Island.

Now Captain Richey is catching up to two more ships from the fleet who somehow made it into the Sound before KANE arrived. It is starting to get dark, but traveling at night really doesn't mean anything to a modern submarine. Even the high-tech Photonics Masts are equipped with light amplification to be able to see quite well at night.

"Conn, Sonar."

"Sonar, go ahead."

"Captain, we are now tracking two Japanese ships about 8 miles ahead of us on about the same course and we are closing. They are running side to side in the channel and only moving about 5 knots, kind of feeling their way. The computer has identified them as the heavy cruisers Aoba, I believe on the left and Kako on the right."

"Sonar, Aye."

The OOD said, "Captain, the Statistician verified the ship names and also added that the Aoba is the Flagship of the Cruiser Division 6. The next in the Japanese chain of command."

"OOD, load tubes 1 and 2, open outer doors, make your depth 90 feet, raise the masts and reduce speed to 5 knots."

"Aye, Sir."

"Photonics, turn on the light amplifiers and give me bearing and range to the cruiser Aoba on the left."

"Captain, Photonics recommend bearing 1-6-5, range 5.6 miles. They are making it easy with their searchlights on."

"OOD, steer course 1-6-5, set torpedo 1 for automatic sonar location and give it the coordinates, set its speed to 50 knots range 7 miles. Whenever possible, Flagships always come first."

With a chuckle, the OOD said, "Aye, Sir".

"Captain, tube 1 is ready. Photonics and Sonar confirm bearing and distance."

The Captain then yelled, "FIRE One!".

Another big Mark 48 torpedo popped out of the tube and tore through the water heading for the stern of the heavy cruiser Aoba.

The Captain was thinking, "Traveling underwater in the late evening, there would be no warning at all. At 50 knots, the speed of that torpedo would give them less than 1 minute to warn the bridge even if they did see it. It just would not happen. Surprise!"

About 5 minutes more of the thick tension went by and then they felt the slight shudder from the impact and explosion.

"Conn, Photonics."

"What do you see?"

"Sir, the torpedo hit the Aoba in the starboard side of its stern. It appears to have removed much of the stern and the ship immediately began taking water and going down stern first. Major fires in the whole stern area, although it is still coasting forward slightly."

"Photonics, bearing and range to the other cruiser?"

"Conn, Photonics recommend bearing 1-7-1, range 6.1 miles and their speed is increasing now to about 8 knots. Their searchlights are looking astern but no way they can see our masts."

"OOD, steer course 1-7-1, set torpedo 2 for automatic sonar location and give it the coordinates, set its speed to 50 knots range 8 miles."

"Aye, Sir".

"Captain, the tube 2 is ready. Photonics and Sonar confirm bearing and distance."

The Captain then yelled, "FIRE Two!"

A special delivery was on its way to the heavy cruiser Kako. The Captain looked at his Chronograph and timed the 6 minutes, 42 second run time.

He heard the ring and pointed to the watch just as the shudder in the water was felt.

"Photonics, report."

"Captain, torpedo 2 hit the Kako about 50 feet forward on the port side. It appears to have blown out a large piece of the hull plating on the side. The ship is on fire and already listing to port and sinking by the stern. The two fires are making it look like daylight out there."

"Conn, Photonics."

"Go ahead."

"Conn, we appear to have created a problem, both ships were still moving after they were hit. The Aoba went to the port and the Kako went to starboard. They're both partially submerged with about 150 feet underwater and about 200 feet apart. Explosions are throwing huge pieces into that gap between them. The result is two 600-foot-long ships with a 200-foot separation has effectively blocked 1400 feet across the channel. Sir, I am also seeing another cruiser coming down behind us."

"Photonics, Aye".

"Sonar, Conn."

"Sonar, Aye."

"Sonar can you tell if that is the Tenryu, coming down behind us?"

"Sir, there is a lot of noise in the water, but I believe so. The computer is having trouble pulling the signature out of all the explosions and cracking of the two cruisers."

The XO looking at his terminal said quietly, "The Tenryu carries triple torpedo launchers, with two centerline-mounted Type 6 21-inch launchers. Plenty to damage us."

"Sonar, Conn."

"Sonar, what can you tell about the rest of the channel ahead?"

"Captain, it doesn't seem like we can go under the cruisers and the side of the channel gets shallow fast. I do believe that a smaller surface ship like the Tenryu could get through beside the cruisers on the starboard side of the channel. We can't unless we run on the surface."

"Sonar, Aye."

"Navigation, Conn."

"Navigation, Aye"

"Navigator, plot a course out of the New Georgia Sound and into the Solomon Sea?"

"Let me look, Sir."

A short delay as the Navigator zoomed in through the on-line charts finding a detailed navigation chart so he could check the depths, at least how they were in 2025.

"Conn, Navigator."

"Go ahead."

"Captain, it appears that we can make a sharp turn around the end of New Georgia Island a small island called Peava. Once we are in the Solomon Sea, we are clear to turn toward Savo island."

"Navigator, what is the course for the first leg of that?"

"Captain, recommend course 2-6-5, but I would advise keeping the speed down and having Sonar watch the course until we get to the Sea."

"OOD, lower the masts, close the tube doors, reload tubes 1 and 2, steer course 2-6-5, make your depth 120 feet, speed 15 knots. Notify Sonar to watch for problems since we are not in a channel."

"Aye, Sir.

THE SOLOMON SEA

August 8, 1942, Time 22:49, in the Solomon Sea,

81 miles west of Savo Island

The Captain had the XO take command for a couple of hours and went and had some chow and tried to relax. Nothing wrong that a couple of cups of mess coffee didn't fix. The boat has been taking a detour into the Solomon Sea avoiding the traffic jam it created in The Slot by damaging two Japanese heavy cruisers. That makes a great strategic roadblock but blocked their path too.

The Captain is thinking, "This will give us a unique approach to the battle at Savo Island. We will be approaching from the west. We need to examine the historic activity on this side of the island."

The captain stopped at his cabin to talk to Chief Petty Officer McClennan about the history.

"McClennan, I am sure you have heard that we disabled the heavy cruisers Aoba and Kako. Unfortunately, that blocked our channel through the New Georgia Sound where we could run submerged. Good for a strategic blockade, but it is making us take a detour through the Solomon Sea. In a few minutes, we will be turning east to approach Savo Island from the west. What does history say is going on in that area now in the early morning of August 9th?"

"Sir, this is the ideal timing. This is about the time when that Japanese Task Force was to get to Savo Island. Since there is only one ship left, who knows what they will do. I can only guess it will not be a major attack on the Allies. There is a group of four Allied ships coming north on the west side of Savo. In history, they were met by three cruisers that don't exist anymore. Another Allied force of five ships is coming north-east of Savo. At 02:00 in history, the Japanese Fleet turned north-east looping around the east side of Savo to run and hide, till dark. As they rounded, Savo to leave the Chokai was hit by Allied fire. Damaged but it eventually met up with the task force again as they passed the USS Ralph Talbot's patrol position. My only suggestion is that we try to find that other cruiser and go after it."

"I agree, Chief, good plan. Thanks."

The Captain headed for the Control Room.

"Captain has the Conn."

"Sonar, Conn."

"Sonar, Aye."

"Can you get a fix on the USS Blue it is supposed to be positioned as a radar picket, north-west of Savo?"

"Sorry Sir, there is a lot of noise. The computer has a ship near that position but I don't have a signature for the USS Blue. So, I am not sure what that ship is."

"Conn, Aye."

"Navigator, plot a course to take us south of the patrol area of the USS Blue, as far north from Guadalcanal as possible to a point west of Savo Island. The Statistician can tell you where we think BLUE is patrolling."

"Captain, I will get that for you in a couple of minutes."

The Navigator flipped through the on-line charts and plotted the location that the Statistician gave him for the USS Blue. Then he was able to plot a course.

"Captain, Navigator."

"Navigator, go ahead."

"Sir, recommend course 0-8-5, distance 81 miles."

"OOD, steer course 0-8-5, ahead flank, depth 150 feet."

"Aye, Captain"

The Captain wrote out another message:

> "To: Admiral Richard K. Trainer, HMAS Australia
>
> SCORPION has cut through the edge of the Solomon Sea and is approaching Savo from the north-west at a distance now of 81 miles. Notify all Allied ships that we are going to intercept the light cruiser Tenryu as they come down the western side of the slot approaching Savo. Order the Allied ships to avoid that area. Also, because the rest of the task force has been eliminated, they should concentrate on watching to the north-west in case we do not get to the cruisers.
>
> Captain of Scorpion."

The Captain again asked the XO to have the message sent.

The boat was 'flying' through the Solomon Sea doing an amazing 31 knots and silent as a Sea Bass.

◆ ◆ ◆

The Captain looked at his Chronograph it had been two hours at Flank speed.

"OOD status please?"

"Captain, we are 15 miles west of Savo Island, current course 0-8-5, at flank speed."

"Officer of the Deck, reduce speed to 5 knots, maintain course.

"Aye, Sir."

"Sonar, Conn."

"Sonar, Aye.

Sonar, what do you have?"

"Sir, I am tracking several ships. The radar picket, what I think is the USS Blue is at bearing 3-4-5, distance 5 miles, moving west. I think the Japanese cruisers Tenryu is on bearing 0-0-1, range 25 miles. I am also tracking the heavy cruiser USS Chicago coming almost directly at us, bearing 1-7-5, but only at 5 knots, range 9.8 miles."

"Sonar, Aye."

The Captain said to the XO, "Damn they must not have gotten the message."

"Ok, I need to get a look. Officer of the Deck all stop make your depth 90 feet, and raise the masts. Photonics, get a fix on the Japanese cruiser."

"Aye, Captain."

As the masts broke the surface the Photonics officer immediately focused on the cruiser Tenryu.

The Captain said, "XO, for a light cruiser, this Tenryu has some guts. Under the same conditions, I would have been heading the other way."

"That is for sure, Sir. Don't know if it is guts or stupid, but they are sticking in the fight."

"Conn, Photonics"

"Go ahead.

"Captain, the cruiser Tenryu at bearing 3-3-5, range 20.5 miles and closing."

"Officer of the Deck, steer course 3-3-5, open outer doors, set torpedo 1 for automatic sonar location, and give it the coordinates, set its speed to 50 knots, range 22 miles. I don't want to overshoot it in this area."

"Aye, Sir".

"Captain, the torpedo is ready. Photonics confirms bearing and distance."

The Captain then yelled, "FIRE One!"

"Conn, Sonar."

"Go ahead."

"Captain, the cruiser suddenly slowed almost to a stop. I think they saw the Chicago. The Chicago is still heading into the target area. Our torpedo is still running hot, straight and normal and the on-board tracking is making up for the change in the speed of the cruiser. Contact in 18 minutes."

"Radio, Conn."

"Radio, Aye."

"Radio, see if you can contact the USS Chicago. Try voice first. Notify them that Scorpion is in the area and they should head away on course 1-2-5."

"Conn, Photonics."

"Go ahead."

"Sir, the CHICAGO is heading right into the torpedo's path. Luckily, they are moving slowly about 3 knots. They have started to exchange fire with the Tenryu."

"Conn, Radio"

"Radio, go ahead."

"Conn, I got through to the USS Chicago. The radio operator gave the message to the Captain. The captain sent back what is Scorpion? Apparently, Captain Henry Booker never got the information from the Admiral. What should I do, Sir?"

"Radio, we should be close enough now to get the Admiral's ship directly on voice. Call them and tell them this is an urgent message for the Admiral, 'Scorpion is engaging the Japanese cruiser west of Savo Island. The USS Chicago is coming too close to the action and is in danger. Please order them away, immediately!'"

"XO, I sure hope the CHICAGO can tell where the torpedo is going and not think they are the target. I really don't want to be chased by an American cruiser, even a 1942 cruiser."

"Yes Sir, I agree."

"Sonar, Conn status report."

"Sir, torpedo 1 is running hot, straight and normal, course 3-3-5, speed 50 knots, range 8 miles."

The Captain did a quick calculation in his head and set his Chronograph for 8 minutes, 21 seconds.

"Conn, Photonics."

"Go ahead."

"Sir, the CHICAGO is turning around and beating it out of the area. It seems to have taken a little damage, but is moving well."

The Captain's watch rang, just then.

"Conn, Photonics."

"Photonics, what do you have."

"Sir our torpedo 1 hit the Tenryu, about 200 feet back from the bow on the starboard side. From the fireworks, I would say we got another ammo magazine directly under their forward guns. They appear to be taking water, going down fast at the bow, and dead in the water."

"XO, I need to send one message then let's get the hell out of here."

"Radio, Conn."

"Radio, Aye."

"Radio, send a message to the USS Quincy, say 'This is Scorpion requesting an update on your status?'"

It took a couple of minutes for the Radioman to get a voice connection to the QUINCY. Then he said,

"Conn, Radio."

"Radio go ahead."

"Sir, the QUINCY must have gotten the message from the Admiral they answered very quickly. Their radio operator read the message to the Captain. His response was:

> *"My best regards and thanks to the Captain of Scorpion. The Quincy took a bit of damage at Guadalcanal, but we are well. Patrolling south-east of Savo Island, no action at this time.*
>
> *Captain Henry S. Anderson., Commanding USS Quincy"*

The Captain out loud but quietly said, "Thank God for that change in history."

♦ ♦ ♦

"Navigator, plot a reverse course back out into the Solomon Sea."

"Captain, recommend course 2-6-9."

"Officer of the Deck, steer course 2-6-9, lower the masts, close the tube doors, speed 15 knots, make your depth 190 feet."

"OOD you have the Conn."

"Aye, Sir OOD has the Conn."

LAND ACTION

August 9, 1942, Time 12:03, in the Solomon Sea,
heading north-west currently 151 miles west of
Savo Island.

After quickly leaving the battle area on Savo Island, the Captain asked the XO to come to his cabin. They walked in and Chief Petty Officer McClennan kind of jumped.

The Captain said, "Keep your seat Chief. We need to talk. Gentlemen, I think it is too dangerous for us to try to cruise around near Savo island any more. We have eliminated the eight ships that the Japanese sent in the Fleet from Rabaul and Kavieng into the battle at Savo Island. That should free the Allied ships to go protect the landing support ships. Maybe that extra protection will make a difference in that battle. Hundreds of brave men have already been saved in this action so they can move on to what this version of history brings them.

We are down to four torpedoes, three of them in the aft room. That plus the poor communication we are having with the fleet is why I have moved back out into the Solomon Sea. The last thing I want is to have an Allied ship engage us because they don't know or believe who we are. However, we were ordered to use all the facilities we have against the Japanese. Chief, where were the Japanese held land bases?".

"Sir, I haven't been looking at that while I was focusing on the ocean battles, give me a half-hour and let me find out."

"All right, XO lets go to the Wardroom for coffee and see what other goodies they might have."

"Excellent idea, Sir."

So, they left McClennan to his research.

◆ ◆ ◆

The Captain and the XO sat in the Wardroom. Both of their thoughts started to go back to the question if they will ever see their loved ones again. The XO is also married. He and his wife Betty have only been married for 5 years. They have been trying to have a child, but have had no success. His deployments are fighting that project. Navy men do not live a normal life.

Just then Lieutenant Commander North walked in. The Captain signaled for him to join them. The Captain said, "Commander North are you starting to feel a little better about what we have done.".

North said, "Well sir, yes and no. With your guidance, we did well in those engagements. My problem really is the things we don't know. What the heck have we done to life in our time? Thousands of people have been touched by our change to history. What does that mean? Are our families even still there? Oh, Sorry Sir. I am just having trouble wrapping my mind around this.".

"That's alright Commander we are all having some of those problems. Keep it together and do your job. We may have something for you to work on real soon. We will find out what all this history change means as soon as we can."

After a little rest and some executive talk with the Commander in the Wardroom, the Captain and the XO walked back into his cabin. The Captain asked, "McClennan, what do you have?"

"Sir I understand where your thinking is going. We have a lot of capability for land attacks too and why not use it.

However, in searching around what the history says about August 9th during the land battles at Guadalcanal, I'm seeing mass confusion. History records the major errors made by a couple of the commanders. Since 1942, military historians have basically torn the facts apart to find blame on someone, and a couple of Admirals and Generals were named in numerous articles. I even found why the USS Chicago was sailing into danger. Their Captain Booker had ordered the Radar and Sonar turned off because he was afraid it would give up his position, he couldn't see the Japanese, let alone us.

All of that leads me to be very cautious about recommending any target in the middle of the fluid action. We wanted to change history, but not destroy an Allied stronghold that was just taken and we didn't know."

"That is very true, so what is your idea?"

"Sir, as you recall the fleet, we have now destroyed originated in Rabaul a major Japanese base. I also found a historic record that after the battle at Savo Island the now late Japanese Admiral Mikasa released the four cruisers, also now dead to return to a base on Kavieng. That confirms where the other part of the Fleet came from. I spoke to the navigator. Kavieng is about 644 miles from our current position. Rabaul is about 495 miles. I would suggest them as targets."

The Captain asked, "XO, what do you think?"

"Sir, I agree. They are targets without the danger of hitting Allied troops and are strategic bases for the Japanese fleet. What the heck maybe we aren't done with them yet."

"I agree too. Thanks, Chief. Ask the Navigator to plot those two points and try to find in history exactly where the naval bases where located in those cities and draw a bullseye on them. I want to deliver the 1000 lb. explosive right in their laps. XO, let's go to control and start to set this up."

"Aye, Captain."

As they walked into control the announcement was, "Captain has the Conn, XO in the Conn."

The Captain said, "Officer of the Deck, status please?"

"Captain, we are 151 miles north-west of Savo and we are patrolling that area, depth 180 feet. Awaiting new orders."

"OOD ask the Weapons Officer to come to the Conn."

"Aye, Sir".

Navy command likes to staff a new high-tech boat like this with experienced and higher-ranking officers. The USS Joseph KANE's Weapons Officer is Lieutenant Commander William North. He is 35 years old, very slim with black hair, a good-looking officer. He is a graduate of the Naval Academy and has served on three of the most recent nuclear attack submarines. He is a specialist trained for years in the technical operation of the advanced weapons systems being deployed in these new boats. Unfortunately, not trained for any of this and it has been getting to him. This plan will keep him occupied for a while.

As he walked into control he said, "Commander North reporting as ordered, Sir."

"Weps, first I want to commend you and your team for the excellent operation in the torpedo battles we just experienced. However, the XO and I believe that since we have been ordered to use all of our facilities against the Japanese. All things considered; I don't think this time in history would be a good time to use a tactical nuke, even if we had one. However, maybe we should use a couple of those shiny white Tomahawk missiles we are carrying. Now, this is going to be a bit of a challenge. As you know in 1942, they didn't have satellite communication or GPS. So, the question is, can we fire a Tomahawk at a target and hit it just based on map coordinates?"

"Sir, one of the Tomahawk variants we are carrying is the Block IV. It is a land attack bird with a very powerful strike controller. Its normal mode is GPS controlled navigation with the strike controller communicating to the boat via satellite and making adjustments, even able to change targets in flight. Unfortunately, we are not going to have communication with it for much more than 20 miles without the satellites. What I am going to need to do is kind of knock it back to basics. Scan a very detailed terrain contour map and feed that into the GPS system as if it got it from the GPS network. To answer your question; Yes, we can fire it and hit a target. However, it will take me some hours to reeducate it.".

"Weps, the historic Statistician, and the Navigator are working on very specific target map coordinates. The targets, in general, are Rabaul and Kavieng. Get your team on those missiles, get ready to fire the VPM Vertical Launch Tubes and let me know when we're ready. Take your time and get it right. I will move us closer so we have an easier flight path."

Weps acknowledged the order and left the control room.

The Captain was reviewing in his mind, "The VPM can be used for a number of functions. In this case, it is set up for launching a Tomahawk Cruise Missile vertically. After accelerating vertically its guidance system will turn it level as it spreads its wings and guide it to the target at 50 to 100 feet off the ground. This Block IV Tomahawk has a range of 900 nautical miles or about 1000 miles, flying at Mach 0.74 or about 550 mph. It delivers a 1000 lb. blast/fragmentary warhead. Needless to say, a formidable and nasty weapon.".

"Navigator, Conn."

Navigator, Aye."

"Navigator, plot an open ocean course to take us north in the Solomon Sea, to get us a bit closer to the targets we discussed."

"Sir, recommend course is 3-1-6."

"Officer of the Deck, steer course 3-1-6, speed 22 knots, make your depth 280 feet."

"OOD, Aye"

"XO, we have 10 hours plus till we get to where I want to fire the missiles and we have to wait for the weapons modifications. I will be in my cabin. I will release the Chief to return to normal duty. You have the Conn."

"Aye, Captain. XO has the Conn."

The Captain walked down to his cabin thinking, "A strange idea just popped into my head. In the middle of all the action, we really have not taken time to see if there are any effects of being transported through time. Not only that but we have made some major changes to history I need to do some checking."

He opened the door to his cabin and saw Chief Petty Officer McClennan reading one of his naval history books. He said, "Chief, I wouldn't believe what you read in that book anymore. I have no idea what it means but I know there have been some big changes to it. I appreciate the good job you did to keep us on track with history. You can return to your normal duties; we are out of the historic area. We are going to change history one more time by blowing the hell out of the Japanese naval bases at Rabaul and Kavieng, as you suggested. Thanks again. You can have the book if you want it, I have another copy. Maybe make new notes in the margin.", the Captain chuckled.

"Aye, Captain."

The Captain picked up his internal phone, pressed a button, and said, "Doctor this is the Captain, please come to my cabin.".

The special guest on KANE is Dr. Alfrid Mershon. He is an interesting story. He is a German man about 55-years-old, with a Ph.D. in Physics along with his MD. That's why we always call him Doctor. He is actually a civilian contractor. He has been involved in a government-funded study on the impact of nuclear power on the crew of a Virginia Class submarine, due to a new form of reactor being used. He is a very well-read and highly educated man even said to be at the genius level. He is not a Navy man and his only job on the boat is to be sure the crew stays healthy and monitor them for radiation exposure. The rest of the time he documents his findings and does research. Kind of strange during an active patrol, but that's the government.

In a few minutes, the Doctor knocked on the door and the Captain invited him in and offered him a seat. Then he started to explain, "Doctor, you know that we have been pulled back in time to 1942. We have also made some major changes to history. I was wondering if there had been any impact on the crew?"

"Captain, first, I believe you know that I have researched and written several papers, books, and research studies on the subject of Time Travel. I have my own interpretation of Einstein's theories, so this is a unique opportunity for me. I have read a lot of Sci-Fi about time travel. Many stories talk about the time paradox. As far as I know, there has never been any proof of that. Actually, there has never been any proof of Time Travel. As I understand, those theories are based on the concept that time is almost a liquid. A paradox in 1942 would cause a wave to travel through time making all kinds of changes to some invisible fluid timeline. I feel I have a pretty fair understanding of the theories about the space-time continuum, but I don't believe that explanation.

I support a theory that has been around for years and been used in its fair share of Sci-Fi works too. It is just a theory because up until today, I didn't think time travel was actually possible. The basics of my theories are the idea of an *Alternate Reality*. I believe we live in a reality, kind of a time bubble. There are many, many more that we are not even aware of. Each reality has followed its own timeline. Some may be very close to ours with a POD (Point of Divergence) which only made a small number of changes. Other realities could be as different as Japan won the war and even defeated the Nazi forces.

So, I don't believe in time travel, I believe in jumping realities. One reality might say that the Five Sitting Ducks were Japanese. Regardless of what you believe, we may very well be the first group to experience it, or maybe not? How could we know?".

"So, Doctor, you believe that our journey back here to 1942, will not be seen in our 2025 reality because we will not be in our 2025 reality anymore?"

"Yes Captain, that is essentially my belief."

"You are right, one way or another we will see. Back to the question. Have there been any physical effects on the crew from us coming back here in whichever reality?"

"Captain, we have had some issues. A few fights some severe stomach distress and headaches. All those I believe are stress-related, nothing I would attempt to blame on time travel. When you think about it, how would our bodies or minds know what happened? Right now, we are all trapped in this big can and have no reference to, let's say World Time."

"Thanks, Doctor, I appreciate this impressive information. Let me know if anything does show up in the crew."

"Yes, Captain."

The Doctor stood and left the cabin.

The Captain was thinking, "That man is brilliant. I wish I really understood all that, but we sure will see it happen."

The Captain looked at his Chronograph, "We have over 6 hours till I want to fire the Missiles, I need a nap.". So, he set the alarm for 5 hours and laid down on his bunk.

MISSILE LAUNCH

August 9, 1942, Time 22:55, in the Solomon Sea,
heading north-west currently 250 miles south of
New Ireland

The alarm went off on the Captain's Chronograph. He just realized that amazingly he had again slept well for 5 hours. When he entered control there was the normal announcement.

"Captain has the Conn."

"OOD what's our status?"

"Captain, we are about 250 miles south of New Ireland, speed 22 knots, depth 280 feet.".

"Weapons, Conn."

"Weapons, Aye."

"Weapons, status of the Tomahawks?"

"Captain, I was just about to call. They have been modified and loaded with high detail, ground contour, map data. They are ready in the Vertical Launch Tubes 1 and 2. Tube 1 addressed to Rabaul and Tube 2 for Kavieng. We are ready to go."

"Very Well."

"Officer of the Deck, make your depth 90 feet, speed 5 knots, raise the masts, steer course 3-5-5."

"Aye, Sir."

"Officer of the Deck, open the VLT outer doors on tubes 1 and 2, arm the Tomahawks."

"Aye, Captain"

The crew made all the changes required to launch a pair of Tomahawks. A different part of the Weapons Control station showed two columns of lights, one for each tube. One at a time they lit up green coming up from the bottom as various systems were activated and readied for launch. In a couple of minutes, both columns showed all green.

"Captain."

"Yes, Lieutenant what do you have?"

"Sir, Tomahawks are armed, we are at periscope depth, speed 5 knots, course 3-5-5, VLT outer doors are open. Ready to fire."

The Captain yelled, "FIRE One!"

The Vertical Launch Tubes are only about 40 feet from control so the control people all heard the loud whooshing sound as the Tomahawk blasted itself out of the tube.

"Radar do you have a track on the Tomahawk?"

"Yes, Sir we do, it has leveled off at 75 feet and is on route to the target."

Then the Captain yelled, "FIRE Two!"

The second Tomahawk blasted out of its tube.

"Radar, report?"

"Captain, Radar, this bird has leveled off at about 90 feet and is on its course too."

"Navigator, plot a high-speed course south of New Ireland out into the Pacific."

"Captain recommend course 0-6-5."

"Officer of the Deck, close the launch tube doors, retract the masts, make your depth 170 feet, steer course 0-6-5, ahead flank."

"Aye, Captain"

The Captain said out loud to the whole control crew, "I sure wish we could stay to see this, but we need to get the heck out of Dodge."

"XO, you have the Conn, I need a coffee."

"Aye XO has the Conn."

♦ ♦ ♦

The Captain went down to the Crew Mess and grab a coffee. Then he went to sit with a few of the enlisted men. He sat down and the men kind of froze. Their conversation stopped immediately.

"How are you men doing?"

No one said a word. The Captain could feel the deep tension among the men. Then he tried to get them to open up.

"Oh, come on tell it like it is."

One young man, Petty Officer Charles Reverie said, "Sir, we are all very concerned about what this all means. We have time-traveled and are in 1942. Now we have made some major changes to history. Thousands of people could have been affected. What does it all mean? Could we have caused a time paradox that destroyed our world, killed our family?"

"Petty Officer, I wish I knew. I really wish I had something more reassuring to tell you. I have never heard of anyone traveling in time for real. Only on Sci-Fi shows and in books. We really have nothing to go by to understand it. We are moving to get out of the war zone and begin to take care of ourselves. We will have to see what we can figure out to try to get back to our time."

The Petty Officer said, "Thanks Captain that made us understand we are all having the same problems."

The others at the table nodded they agreed.

Suddenly, the PA Blared, "Captain to the Conn!"

The Captain jumped up and ran toward control. As he walked in, they announced, "Captain has the Conn."

"OOD, what is the problem?"

"Sir, we are about 40 miles south of the southern tip of New Ireland, course 0-3-5, depth 150 feet, speed 31 knots. As we went past, Sonar reported a Destroyer coming out of Rabaul. He believes it was sitting there quiet and has just started to come out of the channel into the Solomon Sea. It is about 15 miles away and picking up speed."

"Aye OOD, how could they know we are here?"

"They really can't I agree, Sir."

"Navigator, Conn."

"Navigator, Aye."

"Navigator are we clear to turn east if we need to?"

"Sir, not yet. We need to clear Bougainville first."

"Conn, Sonar."

"Conn, Aye."

"Sir, from the sonar signature and some history from the Statistician, I am guessing it is a Kagero Class Destroyer. Just a guess but I think it is the Arashi based on the history of its location on this date in 1942. Top speed 35 knots and heavily armed."

"Sonar, Aye. Let me know when it leaves the channel."

"Aye, Sir."

"Officer of the Deck, just in case lets load tubes 5 and 6, leave the doors closed."

"Aye, Sir."

"Officer of the Deck, make your depth 90 feet and raise the masts."

"Aye, Captain."

In a few minutes, the OOD said, "Captain, depth is 90 feet and the masts are raised."

"Photonics, Conn."

"Photonics, Aye."

"Take a quick look and see if you can get anything on exactly where that destroyer is."

"Sir, from her lights, she appears to be at bearing 2-7-5, range 17 miles. She is just coming out of the channel turning toward us. Her speed is about 30 knots right now and increasing."

"Sonar, Conn."

"Sonar, Aye."

"What is the depth here?"

"Sir, recommend depth to keel 250 feet."

"Conn, Aye."

"Officer of the Deck, retract the masts, make your depth 185 feet, ahead flank."

"Aye, Captain."

"Radio, Conn."

"Radio, Aye."

"Did you get anything while we were at periscope depth."

"Sir, all I got was a partial code message to the Arashi. The message was from Rabaul, telling them of an Allied bombing at the base and instructing them to a codeword hidden patrol sector in the Pacific. No details of that location. I think that confirms the name of the ship and the big boom at Rabaul"

"Radio, Aye."

The Captain asked the XO and the OOD to join him off to the side of the Control Room. Then he said, "Gentlemen, I want your opinions on what to do. My thought is we keep running at flank speed till we reach the deep water in the Pacific. Then make a high-speed turn to the east and dive as deep as we can, still at flank speed. However, if they seem to be following us and closing, we may have to torpedo them, but that will label our position. After what the Japanese saw at Savo, they don't know what sank their ships, but they would know we moved up here. Opinions?"

The XO spoke up, "Captain, I think you are right we have done enough and need to protect ourselves and not engage this Destroyer. We need to remember a Kagero Class destroyer carries the Type 93 torpedo. Not tremendously accurate and with a range about 6.8 miles according to the books. Each one carries over 1000 pounds of explosive; a hit could take us out or at least cause some major damage."

The OOD said, "I agree, let's just get the hell out of here."

The Captain concluded, "Thanks men so that's the plan."

♦ ♦ ♦

Back in the control area, "Captain has the Conn.".

There was an urgent tension in the sonar operator's voice as he said, "Conn, Sonar!"

"Conn, Aye."

"Sir, the destroyer has gone to flank speed 35 knots and they are gaining on us. Range is down to about 15 miles."

"Sonar, Aye."

♦ ♦ ♦

Two and a half hours later, the big boat was again slipping back into the deep blue waters of the Pacific, where it could maneuver if required. They had been watching closely, but the Destroyer didn't seem to know they were there. Until suddenly a sonar report changed that.

"Conn, Sonar."

"Sonar, go ahead."

"Captain, the destroyer is still running at 35 knots. They have now closed to 6.9 miles and still gaining on us. I can't tell but they seem to be following or at least they are on the same course as we are."

"Sonar, Aye."

They are now the fox and the hounds are closing.

"Officer of the Deck, man battle stations."

The claxon sounded and the crew moved.

The Captain grabbed the mike to announce, "All hands this is the Captain. We have just reentered the Pacific. However, we picked up a Japanese Destroyer tailing us, as we went by

Rabaul. They are behind us and now gaining on us. They are now close enough for me to start being concerned about them. We really have no idea if they are tracking us or not. I am about to find out by making a high-speed turn to the starboard. Everyone brace yourself this is going to be the amusement park ride type of turn. Captain out."

"Sonar, what is the depth?"

"Sir, we have just crossed into deep water. Depth 450 feet to the keel."

"Anything else around?"

"No, Sir just the Arashi."

"Navigator, recommend a course to turn east?"

"Sir, recommend course 0-8-5."

"Conn, Aye."

In a bit of a panic, "Conn, Sonar they have fired a torpedo at us. Range 6.7 miles, speed 30 knots, contact in 11.8 seconds."

"Officer of the Deck, steer course 0-8-5 and dive to 300 feet, maintain ahead flank."

Suddenly the boat tilted at a 15-degree angle to the right and went sharply down at the bow. The Pilot and Co-Pilot had to work in synchronized motion with the OOD yelling instructions, to adjust the dive planes to keep the attitude of the boat during this harsh turn. It seemed like the turn took forever with everyone hanging on to whatever they could grab that was bolted down. A couple of coffee cups and clipboards slid off the counter and dramatically crashed on the floor. In 20 seconds, the boat leveled and sped along on its new course at full speed deep into the Pacific Ocean.

"Sonar, Conn."

"Sonar, Aye"

"Can you tell anything about them yet?"

"Sir, the torpedo continued straight ahead on a course about 0-3-7, so far it appears the destroyer is continuing on course 0-3-5, right on past us."

"Sonar, Aye."

"Navigator, Conn"

"Navigator, Aye"

"Plot a course to Bikini Atoll."

"Sir, Recommend course 0-4-5, distance 1086 miles."

"Officer of the Deck, maintain your depth at 300 feet, steer course 0-4-5, speed 22 knots, secure from Battle Stations."

The Captain told the XO, "Let's cruise back to Bikini Atoll and do some research."

"Aye, Sir."

The Captain grabbed the mike, "All hands this is the Captain. Our roller coaster ride did the job. It appears that the Japanese destroyer did track us and fired a torpedo at us. However, our fast turn and dive shook it off and the destroyer proceeded to their patrol sector, after losing track of us. We have set a course for Bikini Atoll to do some research on our calendar problem. Everyone did a great job, get some rest, and some food and we will see what we find on that hunk of radioactive coral. That is all.".

"XO you are relieved. Get some rest and food."

"Aye, Sir."

"Captain has the Conn."

♦ ♦ ♦

Captain Richey is standing in the Conn with his mind wandering back into his own history. He is thinking, "I remember in my early days in the Navy when I served for a few months on a Destroyer. Let's face it most of the time any Navy ship is just cruising in the open ocean. In that surface ship world, you can stand on the bridge and watch the ocean go by.

Looking at white caps rolling by, the wake of your own ship churning up the sea, birds, and dolphins following the ship, the occasional whale all mixed with beautiful sunrises, sunsets, and tropical islands.

The worst part about submarine duty is that it is rare to have time up on the bridge and even when you have that time it makes you feel bad for the rest of the crew. You can't exactly have them stand on the deck of a very round submarine moving at 31 knots with waves breaking over the bow. I guess I will just watch the sonar scope for entertainment.".

BACK TO BIKINI

August 11, 1942, Time 08:30, in the Pacific Ocean,
heading north-east currently 540 miles south-west
of Bikini Atoll

Talking privately to the XO the Captain said, "Mike, let's make sure the supervisors keep on with the short shifts and rest rotation with the men. They all need some sleep and food and we still have a 20-hour cruise to Bikini."

"Aye, Captain. Would you like to take a break now?"

"Yes. I would thank you. I want to go down and see if the Chop has any more of those steaks. You have the Conn."

The Supply Officer, Lieutenant Sam Ramsey, is called the "Chop" because his collar insignia looks like a pork chop. He is responsible for what food is onboard.

"Sir, I am sure when you ask, the steak will appear."

"XO has the Conn."

The Captain enjoyed a fine medium-rare, porterhouse steak, and took a few hours nap in his cabin. He freshened up and change his coveralls always wanting to look crisp as a good example for the officers and crew. That is why he has so many of them and the laundry gives him special fast turnaround. Then he headed back to the control room.

"Captain has the Conn."

"XO what is the status?"

"Sir, we are 420 miles from Bikini, speed 22 knots, depth 280 feet, course 0-4-5. The boat is fully operational. The crew is rotating on short shifts to get some rest."

"Very Well."

"Sonar, Conn."

"Sonar, Aye."

"Sonar anything around us?"

"Sir the only thing I can hear is one ship that has to be 200 miles away, just a strange echo I think because he is pinging too. That and a couple of whales is all I have."

"Sonar, stop active pinging, whales don't like that and we really don't need it."

"Aye, Sir."

"Officer of the Deck, surface the ship. Once surfaced, return to ahead full and send the look outs to the bridge."

"Aye, Sir."

After the ship surfaced the Captain and the XO went up into the bridge to get some fresh air. They looked out on a beautiful sunny day. The ocean looked as flat as a farm pond in a bright shade of azure blue. The sun causing the ocean to sparkle in blinding brightness. The waves rolling over the big boats bow as it slides through the water leaving a white foam in its wake.

The XO said, "Look over there, Sir.", as he pointed to starboard.

The Captain as he saw two white whales breaching the surface with a chuckle said, "There are those whales that sonar was hearing. They came over to check on this ugly fish in their area."

They just stood quietly for a half-hour and watched the ocean go by.

"Conn, Radio."

"Radio, go ahead."

"Sir, I have just translated some Japanese code transmissions being repeated from ship to ship. They are reporting to their fleet a mysterious set of Allied bombings at Rabaul and Kavieng. They said a number of ships had been damaged and the harbors are not accessible."

"Radio, Aye, and thanks."

The Captain had a fake expression of surprise as he said, "XO, I wonder how that happened?"

"Captain, I was wondering that too."

The XO said, "Captain, I am going below and let the OOD come up for a while."

"Good idea."

"XO you are relieved. I asked Chop to keep another steak for you."

"Thanks, Captain, I am starved."

In a few minutes, the OOD climbed up to the bridge and said, "I appreciate this Sir, I haven't been up here for a while. Man, the air is nice."

"Lieutenant, it is a beautiful day. Now, all we need to do is solve our time problem."

"Right, I almost forgot for a few minutes."

In twenty minutes or so the Captain said, "Ok, Lieutenant, let's take it down again."

The OOD commanded, "Look-outs down!".

They all climbed down into control. Then the Captain went down and the announcement was, "Captain is Down".

Next, the OOD came down and announced, "Last man down, the hatch is closed."

"Captain has the conn."

The Captain said, "Officer of the Deck, make your depth 180 feet, speed 22 knots, steer course 0-4-5."

"Aye, Captain."

The Captain grabbed the mike to make an announcement, "All Hands this is the Captain. Men, everyone has done a spectacular job during our entry into World War II in the Pacific. We are in mid-Pacific, heading back to Bikini Atoll. My hope is we can find some way to reverse our time journey and get back to 2025. We have had no reports of any of the Sci-Fi book time paradox effects on the boat. Of course, we don't know if anything has happened back in our world.

The officers and I are going to try to formulate a plan to get us back. If anyone has any technical information that may help, please pass it to your supervisor. No comic book solutions please, they seldom work in the real world. Although, we have never heard of this problem in our world. We still have a long cruise to Bikini, please get some food and rest on the XO's schedule. Thanks again, for the great work. All officers and the Doctor to the Wardroom. Captain out."

"OOD, you have the Conn."

"Aye, Sir, OOD has the Conn."

◆ ◆ ◆

The Officers and the Doctor gathered in the Wardroom. The cook brought out coffee, sandwiches, and snacks and set them on the table, then quickly left. The men all took seats around the long table with the Captain and XO at the heads of the table. After a couple of swigs of coffee, the Captain started, "Gentlemen, I want to congratulate you and thank you and your teams for a fine effort during our visit to World War II. Obviously, the best Virginia Class submarine crew in the battle.".

That gave the Officers a chuckle, they all needed to break the tension.

"We had an advantage with the power of our boat at that time and having a history to tell us what everyone was going to try to do. However, those ships were all armed and dangerous as we found out. They very well could have damaged or sunk us. Even in a battle in our time, eight kills in a battle like that is a pretty good record. Not to mention two naval bases that developed some mysterious explosive problems.

Now we face our other problem. My thought was to address the issue we need to return to where it happened. So, we are cruising back to Bikini Atoll. I have asked the Doctor to attend because he is somewhat an expert in time travel theories. I am open to any suggestions on how to approach returning to our own time."

The Communications Officer Lieutenant Martin Williams, spoke up first, "Captain. It seems obvious that there is no data on a force like we encountered. I have looked at the recording by all the ship's sensors as we passed through that force. Of course, there is a couple of minute gaps when the lights went out. However, it is definitely, radioactive in nature. History tells us they exploded more than 171 megatons of nuclear bombs during the tests at Bikini between 1946 and 1958. Now I am sure the Weps will agree with me that, those tests released a huge amount of various kinds of radioactive fall-out, much of it still there for another 1000 years or so. Especially considering that the bomb that leveled and melted Hiroshima was only 15 kilotons in comparison.

I believe from my research that the field of energy we passed through was at the site of what was called the Baker Test. That test was a 23-kiloton device, suspended under a ship. The result was a huge crater that remains in our time because the sand actually melted. The strange thing is that in 1942 that test has not happened yet. It was done in 1946. However, that one radiation hot spot is there even in this time. That history does explain the high radiation level at that point, but doesn't explain a time warp or the fact that we see it in 1942."

"Thanks, Lieutenant. Anyone else have anything?"

The head of Navigation, Lieutenant Smithy spoke next, "Sir, I have reviewed the data recordings, and the exact location of the field does confirm what Williams said. The contact point was exactly above that crater."

Commander North said, trying hard to sound technical, "I can confirm that too from our sonar recordings I have reviewed. I would also add that the crater is 8 meters deep (27 feet) and 700 meters in diameter (2297 feet)."

Then North continued in a kind of abrupt tone, "My problem is we could make our situation far worse. We have no idea where in time we will end up. I am an educated man but I can't get any hold on what the hell is happening to us. We could have destroyed our whole world and not even know it. The men on my team feel the same way. During the battle everyone was busy. Now they are thinking about the situation just like I am and it is frankly scaring the crap out of all of us. I am sure that a lot of the crew feel the same way."

The Captain thought for a few minutes sipping his coffee. Then he spoke again, "Commander, please calm down. I think we all have the same feelings and issues. It is not like we can look up instructions in a textbook somewhere. This is totally new as far as we know. I am the Captain and I need to lead us to a decision. So, unless you have some solution, let's continue our discussion. Thank you.".

The Captain continued after another sip of coffee and trying to relax, "Men, we have apparently agreed on the where and we know the when we need to work on the what. If we assume that the field, we went through was a result of the

Baker Test blast and the very hot radioactive field at that spot. What could cause a time warp?"

The Doctor spoke next, "Sir, there is nothing in known science or even high-level research that has managed to generate a time warp or time travel, as far as I know. They say that in space they can be the result of a Black Hole because of the huge concentration of gravimetric forces. My theory is that there are many different realities. We are not even aware of the other ones. One might have a timeline where the Japanese lost WWII. Another one might say they won. So, the question is what reality are we in and what reality is our former life in? As for how to get back, I don't know what got us here so I don't know what would get us back."

Lieutenant Williams said, "The only suggestion I can make is that we get there, stand back from that area but study it all we can. Ultimately, the answer may be to try to go through it again.".

The Captain again gave it some thought then said, "I agree Williams, that sounds like a good plan. Anyone object to that approach for any reason?"

The officers and the Doctor all agreed with the idea. Weps agreed with a grumble in his voice.

Assistant Engineering Officer, Lieutenant Paulo Rodrigues said crossing himself, "God help us!"

The Captain concluded the meeting, "Make sure your men get rested up and get some food. During our investigation at Bikini, feel free to speak up with any information or suggestions. Return to your stations. Dismissed."

INVESTIGATE THE ATOLL

August 12, 1942, Time 03:25, in the Pacific Ocean,

5 miles west of Bikini Atoll

Trying to rest in his cabin while the XO had the Conn, the Captain laid in his bunk for almost four hours unable to sleep. Just feeling the motions of the boat. His mind was running at full speed working the many issues, risks, and results of what they might do the next day. In a lot of ways, he felt exactly the same as Weps. However, he knows better than to let the officers or the crew see that. It is his job to be the rock of command. He was also very afraid of the result of what they had already done.

His Chronograph's alarm went off so he decided to go grab something to eat. It was still 03:25 in the morning. He grabbed some food and coffee, then went to sit down. Lieutenant Williams, was already sitting there eating so the Captain said, "Good Morning, Lieutenant. Did you get any sleep?"

"No Sir, not much."

"I didn't either. Just between us, what are your deep thoughts about this problem?"

"Well Sir, I am concerned on one level about even exposing ourselves to that much radiation. The boat is well shielded, but it is like driving through Hiroshima as the bomb exploded. Just not a place you want to be."

"I agree with you, Lieutenant. What else?"

"Sir, we have no idea what that energy field was. However, it is a time portal of some kind. Alternate Reality, Alternate History, or not, we could just as well end up in the Civil War as back in our time. We just have no idea."

"Wow, I hadn't thought of that one. We are really not a boat for that type of fight. Hard to have a modern torpedo home in on a wooden ship and a Tomahawk would send splinters for 5 miles. You have to be entirely too close. However, I don't think a Civil War cannonball would hurt us much though."

A very small smile came to William's face, "Among, other problems, Sir."

"Well Lieutenant, just help me as much as you can. This is far more in your area of knowledge than mine."

"Will do, Sir."

"Well L-T, I need to get back to the Conn. Nice talking with you."

"Thank you, Sir".

♦ ♦ ♦

About 05:00 the Captain got back to Control.

"Captain has the Conn."

"XO, give me a status please?"

"Sir, we are 5 miles west of Bikini Atoll, I have ordered us to patrol here without approaching the Atoll. We are at a depth of 180 feet. In addition, Geiger Counter readings on the hull indicate elevated levels of radiation in the water, about 50 milli-Sieverts but nothing serious at this distance."

"Very Well."

"Sonar, Conn."

"Sonar, Aye."

"Sonar is there anything near us?"

"Sir, no ships for hundreds of miles. However, there is a very loud, strange kind of staticky hum in the water. Not the field we went through but another sound the computer can't identify."

"Conn, Aye"

"Officer of the Deck, make your depth 90 feet and raise the masts."

"Aye, Sir."

"Photonics use all those cameras and fancy sensors to see what you can find."

"Aye, Captain."

The Captain walked over to watch the command center monitor that was attached to the Photonics array. He watched as they scanned the area, first with the high resolution, long-range cameras. Then with the infrared scanners. It didn't seem to him that anything was visible. In a couple of minutes, the Photonics Officer confirmed the same conclusion.

"Navigator, Conn."

"Navigator, do you have a location for the Baker Crater?"

"Yes, Sir."

"The crater is on course 3-5-5 at 4.75 miles."

"Officer of the Deck, ahead at 2 knots, steer course 3-5-5, maintain periscope depth with the masts up."

"Aye, Sir."

"Sonar and Photonics, notify me immediately of any changes."

The Captain was taking the boat in very slowly toward the Baker Crater. In twenty minutes, he got this report.

"Conn, Sonar."

"Go ahead."

"Sir I have started to track a sound that matches what we recorded before we crossed through that high energy field before. As far as I can tell it is right above the Crater."

"Conn, Aye."

"Conn, Photonics."

"Conn, Aye"

"Sir, I can now confirm what Sonar said. I can see that transparent blue sparking field over the crater. We are seeing a horizontal rectangle almost a half-mile long, larger than the last time. The field appears to be moving right to left as if it is the edge of a clockwise circulation. Range about 2.5 miles to the leading edge."

"Conn, Aye."

"Officer of the Deck, all stop. Announce all officers on the communication net please."

The Captain picked up the phone and said, "We have sighted and heard on sonar what we believe is the same energy field that dragged us back to 1942. As Lieutenant Williams suggested it is located directly over the Baker Crater. Site of one of the biggest nuclear tests at Bikini and one of only a couple that were detonated underwater. My current thought is to go ahead and go through it again and see what happens. Having no information to make a scientific judgment, I have to go with a guess. I think we should just jump on into it. Anyone have a better suggestion or objection to that plan?"

No one spoke up as the captain waited a minute or two. Then he said, "Alright I will take your silence as acceptance. Believe me when I say I am not solid with this plan, but I have nothing better. Return to your duties, inform your men, and be ready for anything. Here we go."

"Sonar, Conn."

"Sonar, Aye."

"Sonar, what do your records say our speed was when we passed through the field the first time?"

"Sir, our speed was 18 knots."

"Conn, Aye."

"Officer of the Deck, man Battle Stations, steer course 3-5-5, ahead full make turns for 18 knots. Punch on through the energy field. Let's leave the masts up this time. Photonics and Sonar report any changes."

"Aye, Sir."

The OOD sounded Battle Stations and the entire crew was ready for anything.

The big submarine used all its power and accelerated hard, heading for the energy field. The Captain watched the Photonics screen. As soon as they entered the field, there was nothing but a very bright blue wall with lightning through it. The lights and all of the computer displays flashed off. Then the big blue scanner wall came through control. The same thing was happening as it hit a person they vanished. The Captain was hit and felt the stinging, tingle and then he was back right where he was standing again. The blackout caused

164

everything to reboot, then in a minute, everything was back to normal.

"Conn, Photonics."

"Photonics, Aye."

"Sir, the second we exited the blue field it vanished. Not a trace of it. Looking at the Atoll, I see a beautiful Pacific Island. There are huts near the beach and people walking around and fishing."

"Conn, Aye."

The Captain walked over to the nearest terminal to see this. It was absolutely true. It looked like a beautiful island with farming and fishing going on all over it. A long way from the radioactive hot spot that was there a second ago.

"Conn, Radio."

"Radio, Aye."

"Sir, the entire radio system just came back to life. I have satellite, every communication frequency, and a ton of traffic on all of it."

"Officer of the Deck steer course 2-7-0, speed 22 knots, retract the masts and make your depth 180 feet. Let's get out of here."

"Aye, Sir."

The boat made a sharp turn to port and accelerated out into the open Pacific leaving Bikini Atoll behind.

♦ ♦ ♦

After they had gotten some distance away from where the energy field was, the Captain said, "OOD assume periscope depth, raise the masts, maintain course, speed 5 knots."

"XO you have the Conn. I need to go to my cabin and make a phone call."

"XO has the Conn."

The Captain got to his cabin and picked up his radiotelephone. He told Petty Officer George to connect him with COMSUBPAC.

As he was waiting, he glanced at his watch. Instead of the antique Breitling Chronograph, he saw a far more modern, Breitling Quartz Diver's watch. He thought to himself, "Crap! Maybe there are time paradox effects or is this the Alternate Reality? Whatever the hell happened something changed.".

In a couple of minutes, he was actually able to get through to Pearl Harbor. The person who answered said he was Lieutenant Jones.

The Captain said, "Lieutenant Jones, this is Captain Walter Richey, Serial number 9456322. I am the CO of SSN-809, the USS Joseph Kane a Virginia Class Nuclear Attack Submarine. I need to talk to Admiral John Rankin, Commander of the Pacific Fleet!"

The Lieutenant said, "I am sorry sir but we don't have an Admiral John Rankin?"

"Lieutenant just connect me with the Commander of the Submarine Force Pacific Fleet."

In a couple of minutes another voice answered with a sound of surprise in his voice, "Captain Richey, this is Admiral Henry S. Anderson, Jr., Commander of the Submarine Force Pacific Fleet. Captain, we have you listed as missing in the Pacific with no reports for more than 6 days. What is your report?".

"Admiral, this is kind of a long story but I guess actually we were missing. I think we are going to want to wait till I can explain this to all of the Pacific Command, but let me give you the quick summary. It is hard to even describe this. First, let me ask you a question. What is the date?"

"Captain, what kind of question is that? It is August 12, 2025."

The Captain said, "Thank God, oh sorry Sir. You will know why I asked in a moment.".

"Captain, I have plenty of time give me the summary?"

"Sir, on August 5, 2025, at 09:32 my boat went through a very strong radioactive energy field near Bikini Atoll. Everyone was hit by a bright blue 'scan' that came through the boat, even though we were submerged. As we exited the field, we found we had no radio communication except on the Very Low-Frequency receiver and we could not get any information or orders. Based on a couple of broken Morse code messages and consulting my history book library on World War II; we developed the theory that we had been transported back to 1942 when the landing at Guadalcanal was happening. We decided to go to the Solomon Islands. I assumed I could at least get some communication there. What we found, as I guessed, was that we had been transported back to 1942. The landing at Guadalcanal was ready to start. I was then able to communicate by encrypted Morse code, with the commander of the Amphibious Forces, Admiral Trainer on the HMAS Australia. His orders to us were to use all our facilities against the Japanese fleet which was at

Rabaul, under Vice-Admiral Mikasa. Our mission to help protect the ships at Savo Island.

Because we far overpowered the Japanese Fleet we actually sunk or destroyed all eight Japanese ships in the Fleet. Saving a number of Allied ships that they would have destroyed."

"That's enough Captain! You are absolutely right we need to save this for a Command review hearing. Your story makes no sense at all.

I am going to give you two orders. First, instruct your crew, particularly radio operators, to not mention anything about where you have been or this unbelievable story, to anyone. Cut off all outside communication. Under penalty of Treason charges or something like that and all that can bring. Second, get your butt and that boat to Pearl Harbor as fast as it will go."

"Yes, Sir!"

♦ ♦ ♦

"The Captain hurried back to the Control Room.

"Captain has the Conn."

"OOD, status please?"

"Sir, we are about 35 miles west of Bikini Atoll, course 2-7-0, depth 180 feet, speed 5 knots".

"Navigator, plot a course to Pearl Harbor as direct as possible."

"Conn, Navigator recommend course 0-8-3."

"Officer of the Deck, steer course 0-8-3, make your depth 280 feet, ahead flank."

"Aye, Sir"

The Captain picked up the mike and announced, "All Hands this is the Captain. You will all be glad to know that calendar wise we have made it back to August 12, 2025. There appear to be some major changes resulting from history changing. I really can't tell you how much. We have been ordered back to Pearl Harbor where the officers and I will attend a debriefing by the Pacific Command.

The following order is directly from Admiral Henry S. Anderson, Jr., Commander of the Submarine Force Pacific Fleet. This entire incident is to be considered TOP Secret. Telling anyone about where we have been and what we have done is expressly forbidden. You are now in the ranks of people in the past who have had to keep secrets and take them to their grave. This is at the same level as the Manhattan Project in the 1940s and Area 51 in the 1960s. Anyone who divulges this information will be swiftly Court Martialed on charges of Treason or something equally as serious, which can result in life at Leavenworth making little rocks out of big rocks or the death penalty. Our cover story is that we experienced a severe communication failure that took 7 days to repair and we are returning to Pearl to make permanent repairs. **That is all you can say, ever!**

To ensure secrecy, I am going to instruct the radio operators to block any outgoing communication. If you have a cell phone, don't even turn it on. That is all!".

TELL THE STORY

August 15, 2025, Time 11:09, Arriving at Pearl

Harbor Naval Base

After a long journey across the Pacific, the crew was all dressed in their nicely pressed, summer white dress uniforms. They were standing at attention lining the deck facing to port as the boat cruised very slowly passed the bright white Arizona Memorial. The flags gently blowing in a nice breeze. It was a beautiful day on Oahu. The Captain thought at least that hasn't changed. He and the crew all saluted in honor of the dead from the Japanese attack on Pearl Harbor, December 7, 1941.

From up on the bridge, Captain Richey thought, "I have done this honor many times. This one feels totally different. I have just come back from being in the middle of the war that the attack on Pearl started. A very, very strange feeling. Something big has changed."

The USS Joseph Kane was gently pushed by a tug into its birth at 11:28. The landing crew secured the lines and the shore power connection.

Almost immediately, the Captain received a call from Admiral Henry S Anderson, Jr., "Captain Richey, I want you and your officers to come to the main conference room at SUBPAC Headquarters. We have scheduled a hearing at 14:00. I want your crew restricted to the boat until further notice. I will send a van for you and the officers at 13:30. Captain, bring your history books along."

The Admiral abruptly hung up the radiophone.

The Captain picked up the PA mike, "All officers on the communication net.". In a few minutes, they were all on the conference call.

The Captain said, "We have been ordered to a hearing at SUBPAC Headquarters at 14:00. There will be a van for us on the dock at 13:30. Be there on time! Captain out.". He was obviously not feeling like fun at this point.

At 14:00, they all walked into the hearing room. This is a very big room that looked and echoed like a gymnasium. A beautiful wood floor waxed to death, just no basketball courts. In the center, kind of lonely were two long tables facing each other. A smaller table across the end with a laptop, data projector, and screen. An Ensign was sitting there apparently to run the equipment. NCIS people had taken every recording of any type from the boat and confiscated them, apparently to show to the command here. Then they entirely flushed the memory of history for that period from the boat's systems.

There were armed Master at Arms at every entrance to the room. They had made name tags for everyone, so they all found their seats and stood behind them. The Captain placed his three history books on the table, just as the Admiral was joined by four other Flag Officers at the front table. There was a lot of brass and medals up there. Five highly decorated officers were ready to hear this mystery story. Then the Admiral said, "Be seated.". So, the Officers all took their seats.

The Admiral started to talk. "Gentlemen, the initial information that Captain Richey gave me on the radio, indicates that you have experienced some phenomenon that we cannot explain or even understand. We as the command of the Submarine Force in the Pacific do have to determine the specifics of this entire incident no matter how strange it appears.

Let me remind you that this entire incident is completely Top Secret. Anyone who divulges any information about this incident, will be taken immediately to a Court Martial for treason or whatever charge they can find; possibly punishable with life in federal prison or the death penalty. Do you all get it?".

All the officers loudly and in unison snapped, "Yes, Sir!".

The Admiral picked up a book off his table and walked over to the Captain. He said, "The Captain and I need to talk. There are refreshments in the back of the room, help yourself we will only be a few minutes.".

Now privately, "Captain, you began to tell me a story about how you jumped back to 1942 and destroyed a Japanese Fleet heading for a battle at Savo Island, correct?"

"Yes Sir, that is the capsule summary."

As he handed the Captain a book that was open to a page about the Battle of Guadalcanal, he said, "Captain, please read this chapter."

As the captain started to read this is what he realized, "There was no mention of a Battle at Savo Island. There was only a mention about that area was patrolled by just four Allied ships. In the list was the USS Blue, USS Randolph

Talbot, USS Astoria, and the USS Quincy. It stated they saw no battle action in that area.".

He also read, "They had expected a Japanese Fleet to attack from that direction. However, it was reported that their harbors in Rabaul and Kavieng were destroyed by Allied bombers, sinking several ships and blocking the harbor for weeks. The result was far less resistance to the landings at Guadalcanal than expected and a swift defeat of the Japanese."

The Captain had a shocked look on his face as he put the book down on the table. Then he picked up one of his naval history books and flipped it open to a page marker he had added. He handed the book to the Admiral and said, "Admiral would you read this one."

The Admiral took a few minutes to read about the bitter defeat by the Japanese Fleet at the Battle of Savo Island, including the sinking a number of Allied ships. The Five Sitting Ducks, that included the USS Quincy.

While he was waiting, the Captain looked in the printed log of communication during their time in 1942 and opened to the message he received from the USS Quincy:

> *"My best regards and thanks to the Captain of Scorpion. The Quincy took a bit of damage at Guadalcanal, but we are well. Patrolling south-east of Savo Island, no action at this time.*
>
> *Captain Henry S. Anderson., Commanding USS Quincy"*

As soon as the Admiral had finished reading about the Captain's version of history, the Captain handed him this message.

The Admiral read the short message and it seemed to hit him, more than any of the rest of this unbelievable story. He kept staring at the message and tears came to his eyes.

He said, "Captain, I obviously knew my father was there and he was the Captain of the Quincy. However, the stories he told me were far different than your version and more like my history book. This has given you some serious credibility in my mind. How can we proceed?".

"Admiral, I have one suggestion. An official guest on our boat is Dr. Alfrid Mershon. He has been making a study about the effects of nuclear power on the crew of a Virginia Class sub using the new reactor. He has a Ph.D. in Physics along with his MD. He is actually a civilian contractor. He is a very well-read and highly educated man even said to be at the genius level. He has a great deal of knowledge in the theories of time travel and Alternate Reality. I believe he can help explain some theories in this area.".

The Admiral said, "Captain, that might help because I sure have no ideas."

The Admiral turned to the Ensign at the end of the table, "Ensign, call KANE, and get Dr. Alfrid Mershon over here."

"Aye, Sir."

The Ensign quickly left the room to make the calls and send a car for the Doctor.

The Captain said, "Admiral, may I show you something. The Admiral walked over and the Captain pointed to his watch. When I left, my watch was a beautiful and historic 1942, Breitling Cronomat, Mariner's Chronograph. That watch was a present from my wife, Jean. She found it at a pawn shop, they had no story on it except they were told it was lost in a ship sinking in WWII and found by hobby divers. It had been cleaned and reconditioned. Now it is a much more modern watch. A small paradox, I don't know?"

"I don't either Captain."

In the meantime, the Admiral called the rest of the Officers back to the table.

After everyone was seated again, the Admiral started, "I am sorry for the delay, but I needed to kind of compare notes with the Captain. We have not even begun to investigate any explanation, but it appears we are from different times or realities or something."

There was some quiet whispering from the Officers.

"We are inviting Doctor Mershon over to help explain. It seems that he has had some scholarly experience in this area and might help us make sense of this. While we wait, Captain please pass my history book to your Officers. Gentlemen, please read that chapter, then we will talk." He had also taken the Captain's book to share with the Flag Officers.

While they waited, each man read the book and you could see the shocked expressions move down both of the tables with the books.

In a few minutes, the door at the end of the room opened. The Ensign showed the Doctor in and added a chair for him in the middle of the Officer's table.

The Admiral said, "Welcome Dr. Mershon. Please read the chapter in that book the Officers have.".

The doctor quickly read the book.

Then said, "Admiral, we have a big problem don't we."

179

The Admiral said, "That sir is an understatement for sure.

Doctor, how do you propose we proceed to evaluate this condition?".

"Admiral, I grabbed one of my presentations on this subject and gave it to the Ensign. If we can look at a few of those slides, I believe it will help, at least with our understanding of my theories."

For the next hour, the Doctor explained his theory of an Alternate Reality or Alternate History. Although no one really understood his theory in detail, they could understand the concept and the Doctor's charts helped. The result is that this USS Joseph Kane and crew actually came from another reality where they destroyed the Japanese Fleet at Savo Island in 1942. It joined this reality at this time in 2025. In this reality, there was never a battle there and the ships like the USS Quincy patrolled a sector with no real naval activity, while the Battle at Guadalcanal did go on.

Then the Doctor said, "Admiral, let me ask you some questions."

"Fine Doctor, go ahead."

"Admiral, was there a USS Joseph Kane, nuclear submarine before we showed up?"

"Actually, yes there was. It had been ordered to investigate some strange reports in the area near Bikini Atoll."

"Admiral, is there still only one USS Joseph Kane?

"Yes Doctor, in fact, I had fleet operations check that this morning. Your boat is it. The other one had been missing for 7 days till your Captain called in."

"Admiral, was the crew roster the same as the one our Captain gave you this morning?"

"Yes Doctor, it was. What the heck does that mean?"

The Doctor started to summarize, "This is one part of the story that I can't explain. Well not the only part. It appears that in this time reality, the USS Joseph Kane, existed along with all of the same crew and the boat was missing for 7 days. Our return somehow replaced the ship and crew in this reality an exact match and instant replacement. My imagination, not science tells me that the two realities must have bumped in some way. They shared a common element for a period of time, our ship. I can't explain that with any of the time theories. It is almost like a leakage between two reality bubbles. Like you see sometimes between two soap bubbles. Maybe even we were living in both. I can't say how long the leakage lasted."

The Admiral said, "Thank you, Doctor. I think that before we try to resolve the reality differences, we as the Command of the Submarine Forces in the Pacific, need to hear your version of history. Captain, it's your show."

For the next three hours, Captain Richey, assisted by the Ensign, walked through the logs of the entire voyage into history. They showed some amazing video from the Photonics Masts and played some very strange audiotapes of code and audio transmissions and screen videos of the computer translating the code. Pictures and sounds that a 2025 boat had no business ever recording. He discussed his orders and his decisions and why he engaged that fleet. Some of the other officers supported his story and the decisions he made. North decided it best to shut up. The Captain also explained the cruise missile attack on Rabaul and Kavieng. Possibly explaining the mysterious bombing reported in the Admiral's book or maybe not?"

Once it was all done, the Admiral said, "Thank you, Captain. Now I think we understand what you all experienced and it seems to be completely real. Although at this point, I am not sure what that word means. Doctor, do you have any idea how we can explain this or what we should do?"

"Admiral, I have had and been working on these theories for 10 years. Until 10 days ago that is all they were is theories. I think if I had unlimited funds and ten more years, I <u>might</u> come up with a good explanation and a way to reverse the problem. However, the more I think about that, I believe that might even make things worse. No one knows what happened in our old reality after we made such a huge impact on the timeline in that particular sphere of time. A very large number of individual timelines would have been drastically changed. Thousands of people on both sides and WWII history beyond that point would have all changed. Ships we sunk were players later in the war. Ships we saved would have then moved into conflict later in the war.

I think maybe we just let our crew, this limited number of people, find where they are in this reality and try to move on. It will not be easy for any of them. There can be a wide range of changes, some might be very hard to take. Obviously, there can be family changes, people who no longer exist, and much more."

The Admiral responded, "Doctor, I think I agree with you. As you explained and what I read in comparison to this timeline, we may have existed in Alternate Realities that were very similar. From the limited information we have looked at here, I can see there was a change in the history of Bikini

Atoll. Yes, there was a Manhattan Project, we did build the two nuclear bombs that ended the war. However, all the bomb testing was done in New Mexico. More liberal parts of the government objected to irradiating that little Pacific atoll and contaminating that entire part of the Pacific. Therefore, not leaving the huge radioactive hot spot, you encountered from your time. The strange thing is that testing was not till after your visit to 1942. The Battle of Guadalcanal was a decisive and quick Allied victory, but the war went on only to end with the nuclear bombs. I believe the differences may be small in comparison to what must have happened in your old Reality. It could have been devastating changes to thousands of people."

The Captain spoke up, "Admiral, I believe we have taken the proper first step. As hard as it may be, my crew must never reveal this story. Actually, if they ever did, it would most likely be taken as a conspiracy theory, like Area 51 rumors were in the '70s.

I think we need to give the entire crew some time to rest and contact their family connections by phone. I think we need to offer them some counseling to deal with what they find out. Then I think we should bring their important family members and children here so they can receive some group help and counsel. I also would like to see some money allocated to help with any serious problem that may have been caused.".

The Admiral looked over at the other Flag Officers who all nodded in agreement with the Captain's proposal. Then the Admiral said, "We agree with that Captain. That is a very thoughtful and fair way to try to help. We will make it so."

After a minute, the Admiral continued, "You will all continue as the crew of the USS Joseph Kane in this reality. Gentlemen, I believe no one in this crew did anything wrong. I can also assure you that the records of this meeting, your interviews with counselors, and all the recordings from your boat, will be locked away in the archives of the US Navy never to be released or declassified. The data storage on the boat has already been scrubbed. I encourage you to destroy any personal records you may have made. You are all dismissed. The van will take you back to the boat.

Captain, I want you to go back in my car. I want to address your crew.".

The Captain and the Admiral walked out to the car. On the drive over to the boat, the Captain said, "Admiral, what did you think about that message I got from your father and the fact that my book shows the USS Quincy's Captain and much of the crew were killed in the original battle?"

"Captain, I think I don't begin to understand. That was the single factor that gave you the credibility to prevent me from just having you and your crew locked up in a crazy farm, for treatment of mass hysteria. However, I thank you for saving my father in your version of Reality."

The Admiral was welcomed on the USS Joseph Kane with all the Navy tradition. The Boatswain piped the Admiral on board and announced, "SUBPAC arriving.". The Captain was announced with, "KANE arriving.".

The Admiral addressed the entire crew in the mess area. He told them that they were not in any trouble, but they had to maintain this, Top Secret information as long as they live and warned them to destroy any personal records or cell phone recordings.

The Admiral arranged for shore leave in Pearl for a month. While the crew relaxed the Navy provided counseling for any crew members who had encountered changes in their family history and could not tell them why or anything about it. There were a few.

Changes but nothing like the Sci-Fi dramas that describe this destructive paradox wave ripping through time. The

Doctor was right that this Alternate Reality was not very far from the one they came from.

The crew all had the opportunity to call their family and friends and then to bring them to Pearl for counseling.

The XO, Lieutenant Commander Michael Mascoll had a major change. His wife Betty started talking to him about his baby boy. He and his wife had been trying to have a child. In this reality, he had one. His wife came to Pearl to meet with him and he had to hide his surprise as he met his son. The XO was a bit upset that he missed the fun but very pleased and of course, couldn't explain his surprise.

The Captain contacted his wife Jean. During the conversation, there didn't seem to be any major changes. Once Jean came out to see him all that he thought was different was her hair color, now a wild "colorful" frosted look. She noticed his watch and said, "What happened to that?"

He responded, "I banged the antique on a metal ladder and broke it and it fell in the ocean, so I had to buy a new watch. Sorry, honey."

Jean responded, "That's OK. You are back, I love you and things are the same.".

The Captain thought to himself, "Well, not really!"

There may be many more incidents of changes, but in the U.S. Navy, no one will **ever** tell you. It will remain another story, locked securely away by the U.S. Government. Right now, it would be easier to find the history of what went on at Area 51 in 1961, than this story about the **USS Joseph Kane** in 2025.

The End!

IN CLOSING

Readers, I enjoyed bringing you this story. I would like to encourage you to post a review of the book on Amazon. Those reviews are extremely important to Independent Authors.

I've written several books on a wide range of subjects. I invite you to check my web site at

TomsBooks

(www.ttrimb1e.com)

While you are there subscribe to my Newsletter

and go to my Author Page on Amazon.

https://www.amazon.com/Thomas-B-Trimble/e/B07JNJ33XL

Special Author's Note: The version you just read of this book was a Second Edition. I am not a Navy man so much of the action and dialogue has been criticized. I have created this new edition to attempt to correct some of those issues with help from several former submarine sailors.

I want to thank my Technical Consultant on this new edition: Retired **CMDCM(SS) Gary Flesher**. That is command master chief petty officer for the rest of us.

He served on the following submarines. He was COB on the USS Nevada SSBN 733G. He also served on the USS Patrick Henry SSBN 599B; USS Patrick Henry SSN 599; USS Hyman G. Rickover SSN 709; USS Georgia SSBN 729G.

Hopefully improving the technical detail will make the book more enjoyable to all. Everyone needs to remember it is a Fiction in a lot of ways. Enjoy the story and theories.

Thanks. Hope to see you again.

Thomas Trimble

ABOUT THE AUTHOR

Thomas Trimble was born in Richmond, VA. He was trained in electronic technology and started to work with Western Electric in 1970. Thirty years later he retired as a Distinguished Member of the Technical Staff with Bell Laboratories.

He has always liked science fiction and the areas of time travel, cyber warfare-espionage, and just major futuristic possibilities in the world of science and computers. Please investigate his library of books covering a wide range of genres.

Made in the USA
Monee, IL
16 July 2020

36623513R00111